MA'SITTER

YOUNG. BLACK. PREGNANT. ALONE

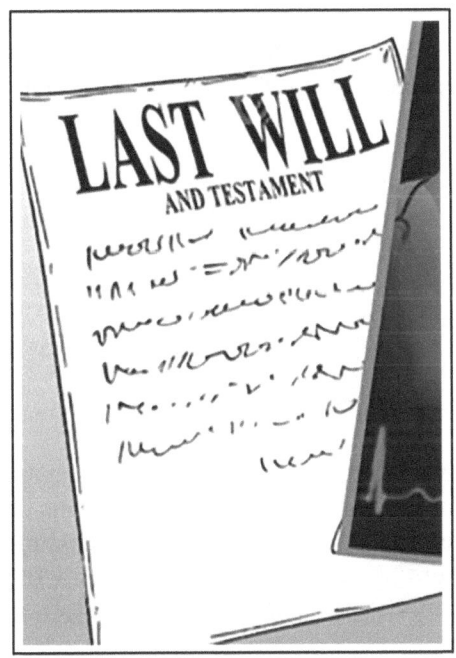

BY

LATOYA LAWSON

MA'SITTER
YOUNG. BLACK. PREGNANT. ALONE

by LaToya Lawson

Dedicated to My:

7/29/85

8/8/01

9/6/04

9/6/04

In loving Memory of
the First Cowboy I
Ever Met

Chaka Nelson

Table of Contents

CHAPTER

ONE

*W*hen I was pregnant, my beloved cousin, Zaka, was killed – shot in the back of the head. His tall frame always stood out in one of his fitted plaid shirts, buttoned to the top. He always wore boots made of real snakeskin and a black cowboy hat with a feather on the left side of it. He also had the largest belt buckle I had ever seen in my lifetime, and I always snickered at his skintight pants. All the boys I ever saw wore oversized pants that sagged.

I learned all of life's real lessons from Zaka, like how to be a boss and always raise my head high whenever I introduced myself. When I was younger, I would spend time practicing how to say my name in front of him.

"Alright. Go," he would say.

I would stand tall in front of him, holding my head as high as I could. "Victoria Dianna Lewis," I said. I grew up in Chicago, so I spoke properly. Whenever I introduced myself to the white families that Grandma Louise cleaned for, they'd always tell me I was intelligent because of it.

"That's right, little cousin. That's how you introduce yourself." Zaka cheered me on no matter what. He had more confidence than a runway model. Zaka could have been a model, as all the girls loved him. Everyone joked around with him by saying he would have babies in every town in Mississippi.

He had the straightest teeth that looked whiter than Clorox bleached clothes. His black, clear, oily, Vaseline skin looked like he wore make-up. Zaka was the man! I took pride in knowing I was his first cousin; now that's real kinfolk. This is how I remembered him.

Zaka never had any babies. All the fast-tail girls, as Grandma Louis would often call us, beat him to the punch. Even me! My daughter, Mona, was born shortly after Zaka was killed. When I saw her face for the first time, I knew something would have to change. I wanted to break the cycle for my daughter, but no matter how I strived to escape the same hood that had slain Zaka, it always located me. Something about that street life clings to my interest, probably because I was good at it.

I was seventeen when I graduated from high school and did not understand what I sought to do with my life. Not one person told me about college; I was clueless and ignorant. Furthermore, I was an unexpected young mother. All I comprehended was what I voiced to Zaka before he died, that I'd be a powerful boss, but what was I supposed to do? I had no guidance, and now, most of the time I was a penniless single mother, as Mona's daddy denied her.

You're a boss. I often heard Zaka's voice in my head. I couldn't go back to a nine-to-five job, but I remembered my cousin Sabrina who made a killing sitting with older white people. She worked for a temp service for many years after settling in Mississippi. Therefore, she knew a lot of people who yearned for their own private sitter, not a temp service one.

Sabrina belonged to the redbone circle of the family. Growing up, the cherry colored ones got favoritism and the blackberry ones, like myself, let's just say we were located outside with a re-used plastic muggy milk jug of water in the scorching summer months in Mississippi.

The cherry ones stayed in the house watching *Tom and Jerry*, *Saved by the Bell* and *All My Children*. Even in school, the cherry ones were always chosen to be in the parades as Mr. and Mrs. 5th grade prom king and queen; the teachers even cherry-picked them to run all the errands, walking through the school hallways gracefully.

We blackberries stayed imprisoned in the classrooms entirely, only prohibited to use the bathroom or maybe get a swallow of water. Sometimes, we had Recess, but who wants to go outside in the heat and get even darker. Not me!

All the boys pursued the cherries, leaving us blackberries as the last option. I just hoped this was not the case when sitting with well-off white people. I mean, they pioneered this mess during slavery by placing the brighter ones in the house and the darker ones in the field.

Zaka told me this, and I experienced first-hand that it was true! I was dark and related to the mistreatment by my own family, community and society.

Sitting? How troublesome could it be? I thought. I'd dealt with way worse shit than sitting with elderly white people, and I used to help Grandma Louise clean homes for loaded white people when I was an adolescent. She had coached me to labor for white families, so I reckoned it would work out for me.

Grandma Louise, as I called her, nurtured and prepared every single woman in the family to work. The matured children called her Mama. She introduced every grandchild to the physical meaning of Proverbs 13:24. "He that spareth his rod hateth his son: but he that loveth him chasteneth him betimes."

Whenever I set out to the tree to pick my own switch, I would hear her say, "Spareth the rod, spoil the child." She was strict, with a permanent mean looking appearance that frightened us youngsters. Grandma Louise was a deep-rooted Baptist whose rules mirrored the Ten Commandments. "Thou shall not Trick or Treat!"

We constantly had a perfect attendance at church. Wednesday night was bible study; Sundays I called, *"Triple C,"* short for three church services, namely First Sunday school, second children's church and then big-adult church. Mama's favorite saying is, "If you party on Friday and Saturday, you can climb your ass out of bed on Sunday."

Yep, she was a cursing Baptist Christian. Sometimes before and after all that churching, she caused hell! Occasionally, she would thump our brittle heads with a black and faded gold-battered, weather-beaten King James Bible, the sixteen eleven edition. "First written edition."

Typical southern grandma.

Grandma Louise fostered a whole heaping of gorgeous blue-eyed snowflake babies and was warmhearted to them, young'uns. Those white families she labored for treasured her. She could have effortlessly secured us a sitting job, cleaning job etc. Grandma Louise bred female workhorses, but she refused to plant her reputation in that field of work for any of us.

My cousin, Sabrina, was different. She referred to anyone hunting a sitting job. Sabrina had the hookup, so it merely took a few days to stumble on my initial sitting job.

They respected the proper speaking Southside of Chicago branded as Chi-Raq's charming Sabrina. She migrated down south years ago with her oversized stuffed bags of extensive city sophistication. Maneuvering in the hearts of many elderly white clients, she established trustworthy relationships. She understood exactly how-to landslide under people's skin despite color. Sabrina's skilled technique unlocked doors for others like me.

CHAPTER

TWO

I started off on the weekends performing private sittings' with an old-fashioned couple, Mr. and Mrs. Bradford. It was boring as hell, but it waged more than Hair Design College back when I was employed there. Plus, my mom agreed to watch after Mona while I worked on the weekends.

Mona arrived into the world swiping hearts; the family's first girl in years stole the show. I didn't have a terrible time coming across family to babysit her if necessary. My chocolate, bald baby girl with the deep jaw dimples, was precious and so adorable. Barely crying for no reason, my baby Mona was a diva.

My baby was like no other, but, instead, like a little woman stuck in a baby's body. I mean she kept her clothes puke-free. My Mama would always sniff around her neck to see if it's sour. I can tally on a single hand the times it stunk. Mona stayed fresh and picture perfect while constantly smiling at everyone. A favorable happy baby.

Contributing me so much inspiration when my 'get-up-and-go motivation' is on empty, Mona launched a sweet whining sound whenever I lifted my sugar up. From daycare or my mama's house, I call it an exceptional mama whining sound. She misses me just as much as I miss her. Someday, I pray to be financially situated to reside "Home sweet home," with Mona "My sugar," entirety.

This would eliminate dropping her off while I grind. Until then, I will cling to my dreams.

My primary full-time client was Mrs. Lane. I cared for her before Mona was eleven months. Finally, having my own client made me feel accomplished; I was informed Monday through Friday, and the nine-to-five case was the schedule. It gets no better than that.

Mrs. Lane was a thin white woman with one grayish-blue eye. The other eye was brown. Her high cheekbones were blushed with rose color and she wore short blonde hair and, awful brown eyeliner with pink-red lipstick to make her lips look fuller. She sported a loose sapphire silk blouse and indigo dress slacks as if she was just coming home from a busy day at the office. In all reality, she was in a wheelchair and couldn't even speak. *"A married man's dream come true."*

On my first day, when I first walked into her home, I was flabbergasted, thinking, it's just like the mansions I pipedream about. Mrs. Lane and her husband shared a two-story home with an enjoyable sunset view from the first-floor deck that was occupied by two dingy mutts.

Just nasty.

Minus the mutts, this place was *"Spot-on goals,"* for a young black girl like me.

Mr. Lane was faintly hunched over as he walked sluggishly, chauffeuring the wife's wheelchair while parading me around their home for the first time.

"This place had the whole shebang!" Gleaming hardwood floors and enormous elevated windows with a modern touch. I developed a hunger for material things like this, so I recognized a lavish property when I saw it. The custom-built kitchen ought to have been a few more smidgeons' bigger. Chestnut kitchen tables surrounded by even darker granite and cabinets decreased the size to the human eye.

I glanced at the multi-colored, busy master suite with an impressive modern-day bathroom. It's the perfect size for the Lane's large, white Jacuzzi tub.

My, my, look at this sunroom, cedar-lined with a hot tub and a huge, brown ring. Guess they're not enjoying that anymore.

The movie theater hadn't been touched. Trash full of molded popcorn appeared months old. I might be a hater. Mr. Lane finished flaunting me around their home. He had little input, giving the impression of a grumpy old man. He had to be over six feet. Mr. Lane's ears bore a resemblance to comical -cartoons. His skin was pale white, and he had wrinkles and tats everywhere. I wasn't accustomed to meeting this class of a white man, and my Grandma Louise did not labor for white husbands like this.

Back when she spick-and-span residences, the white husbands sported double-breasted suits and long-sleeved white shirts underneath. The husbands flexed on the wives with gold-diamond square cufflinks, smelling like big bucks wearing scuff-free brown church shoes. Therefore, glimpsing Mr. Lane's tattoos and basic t-shirt was an eyesore.

After we concluded the tour, it was time to chat about the position. Mr. Lane wheeled Mrs. Lane into the custom kitchen, and I sat at their long chestnut wooden table with a pen and notepad writing down everything he said. Mrs. Lane just smiled and shook her head. She just agreed with everything he said.

In my family, the women didn't shake their heads; they rolled their eyes and necks and pointed their fingers in your face, so this was different for me.

When Mr. Lane was done talking, I totaled the list of duties he gave me as if they were items on a receipt. I told myself if the responsibilities surpassed ten, I wasn't coming back. I had shit to do. Luckily for them, it was no more than seven caregiving requirements.

"Is that all, Mr. Lane?" I asked. I was ready to go.

"Yes, of course, that is all. Not too much is it?"

"No, sir." I grabbed my purse and took out my keys. This was how I let people know that I was ready to go.

"We'll walk you to the door," Mr. Lane said.

And just like that, my first day, even though it was a boring introduction, was over.

As I proceeded towards the front of the door, I sensed Mr. Lane's eyes on my back. I gazed back at him to make certain my senses were dead right.

It was.

I released a slight smile and quickly made my way out the front door. I walked down the brick steps leading out of the house as slowly as I dared to go. The house was all brick and reminded me of a story Grandma Louise told me.

When I was around thirteen years old, she told me about the Ole Miss riot of 1962. She was cleaning a house for another rich white family. The news came through on the family's radio, to which she stopped in the middle of what she was doing, quickly put the mop back in the bucket full of murky hot water and ran outside to sit on their porch. As she sat on their brick porch, tiny goose bumps rose on her arms as she heard about the bricks being thrown during the riot.

I thought maybe Mr. Lane was one of those white men. Hell, he was about fifteen years older than my grandmother, so he fits the age range. Knowing he was that much older than her only made me think.

Maybe he was one of those guys. *Maybe he didn't want me to be here, but he needed someone to take care of his wife for him.* As his eyes pierced the back of my dark-skinned neck, I felt his rage at needing a black woman. His stiff face and body gave his real mood away.

I hauled ass out the driveway as speedily as I could without appearing intimidated.

Later that night, after I bathed and rubbed Mona down with baby lotion, her innocent brown eyes caught my attention. The way she eyeballed me while holding her own bottle with one hand bonded us differently.

I realized she was growing. Once she finished her bottle, I laid her down in her girly playpen, removing each toy.

Wishing she would ease to sleep, I cracked the bathroom door open, watching her while I took a bath. Halfway through my bath, she stood up yelling 'mama'. *Like, hurry up.* Those tight brown eyes of hers pieced my soul again.

I rushed out the tub half washing my body. Mona yelling 'mama' made me eager to feel the warmth of my baby. I dried off, threw my underwear and t-shirt on, then grabbed my baby.

I turned the lights off and snuggled us under the covers. My silk floppy head scarf slipped off while adjusting our pillow. Little by little, I repositioned my arm from holding her until I eased out the bed and flicked the lights on.

Mona's tiny head popped up; she flung the cover back then climbed out the side of the bed, climbing down until her miniature bare feet reached the floor.

Mona stared up at me like, "I am coming, Mommy."

The entire time I was in the bathroom rigging my scarf, my eyes stayed embedded on her. She only had on a onesie; we both sweated at night. Fewer clothes are how we rock. Becoming fonder of motherhood, I grinned as she headed straight my way. Mona started crawling towards me, saying "mama".

I was done fiddling my headscarf and chose to pay attention to her, specifically, to see what she would do. I then glanced at the none-functioning cable box clock to check the time. The box displayed ten fourteen, a Monday work night. "Without warning."

Mona plucked up on the chair. Trembling as she stood up, baby girl wobbled in my direction, reminding me of a drunk. Mona walked to me for the first time. Still on her feet, staggering as she whined 'mama', Mona reached me. I was so overjoyed that I cried, thinking I would have been at work whenever she took her first steps. I praised, kissed and hugged her so tight.

She was just eleven months old. We laid back down and I positioned her on my chest, spoiling her. Once Mona started drooling, it was "night-night", as she says. I shut my eyes as I prayed to God, thanking him for providing me with a better occupation, even though it appeared boring as hell.

With my eyes closed, I tugged my black-and-white comforter over my head. I embarked on a journey fantasizing that the movie theater and custom kitchen at the Lanes' was mine, where I was frying catfish filets and baking three-layer German chocolate cakes in a lighter, bigger custom kitchen. My sunroom had a hot tub, too, and it was clean. The bubbling hot water soothed my luscious body as soapsuds trickled down my blackberry curves. Sipping on a glass of wine, I beamed from ear to ear.

CHAPTER

THREE

*T*he next morning came quickly. It seemed as if I had just shut my eyes and said my prayers. I wasn't used to getting up so early, as I pretty much made my own schedule. When I was enrolling students in barber school, pushing knock-off purses and shoes through the Academy – just to make some washing powder and bologna sandwich with no cheese money.

The Lane's required me at their home based elder care estate at 7:00 in the morning. So, I dropped my baby girl off at the daycare center and sped to work.

When I drove up to their house, Mr. Lane was seated in a white wooden-rocking chair on the well-built porch with their two mutts. He was rocking back and forth, fully dressed in baggy jeans and a black T-shirt that had "Campers and Bikers should be as one" printed on the front in white, chalky color.

"Good morning," he said as I walked up the stairs to the front porch.

"Good morning. How are you, Mr. Lane?"

"I am fine. We had a good night." He kneeled to adjust his dog's collar. I didn't know what he meant when he said that, but I was ready to work, and that's all I focused on.

"That's great, Puma, get on in here with Mrs. Lane now," he said to his mutt.

When we walked in, I laid my purse down and headed straight into the master bedroom to wake Mrs. Lane up. She was lying down in a sleigh bed with a leather headboard trimmed in a cherry wood finish. I guessed she was still sleepy.

She lay there with the green-patterned bedspread tucked around her. The room was pattern for pattern with matching solid green chairs. Apparently, a solid color was a must.

At the entryway of the room, the colors of the walls were unnoticeable. The patterns completely took over the room and its contents. I didn't want to wake her, but we had a busy day, and she was on dialysis.

I leaned over the bed and tapped her softly.

"It's time to get up," I said in a soft voice. She smiled and nodded. I lifted her up and helped her into the wheelchair. She looked so grateful.

When I wheeled her into the bathroom, she was pleased, and I had a hunch why. Mrs. Lane's adult diaper was drenching and reeked of urine. Bedsores indicated this was an ongoing situation. Mrs. Lane should be repositioned at least every two hours being that she's immobile. Sabrina had Certified Nursing Assisting books she made me read and quizzed me on. I had no license, but I still learned how to properly care for patients. I undressed her and lifted her into the shower. Once she was in the shower, she was able to sit in the chair.

Once I turned on the shower, she motioned for me to shampoo her hair. I was puzzled at how she could move her hands and feet, particularly to shower herself. Moving around seemed simple for her, as she moved briskly for a stroke patient.

Something mysterious is going on here.

Once out the shower, I noticed inflamed sores while drying her off. So, I wheeled her back in the room and lifted her onto the bed. Mrs. Lane had an unopened prescription of cream for bedsores. An assortment of bandages merely covered the side bedroom table. Mr. Lane had more than enough to treat his wife's bedsores. I gently cleansed each bedsore, applied a generous amount of cream and bandaged the neglected doll, masking the truth. Her heavyweight diaper was triple bagged.

After massaging her body with lotion, I applied a modest squirts perfume and she showed me how to do her makeup. That terrible tremor in her hands just wouldn't let her do it on her own.

The sweetness I experienced from this retired Barbie Doll made applying her makeup enjoyable. With just her undergarments on, we proceeded into her walk-in closet. She pointed at a solid baby-blue blouse with a bluebird pendant on it. She also selected a pair of navy-blue dress slacks and backless silver sandals with a touch of navy blue. *"Blue must be her favorite color."* I peeked down at her toes and shook my head. She peeked down, too, and giggled. "I must polish those toes before you expose them," I said smiling.

"Where's the nail polish?" I asked. She gestured me to look under the sink in the bathroom. Perhaps, I had a minor 'keep your toes polished' fetish. Light pink is what I selected.

When we were finishing up in the bathroom, Mr. Lane approached, complaining about the time and the fact that Mrs. Lane hadn't had any breakfast yet. He had absolutely no patience. He should be happy, considering his wife was dolled and creamed up.

I smacked my teeth in frustration. "Well, Mr. Lane, I like my clients to be well groomed." This old man would not rush me to do my job. It wasn't like he would groom his wife's toenails. He barely had any sense to change her diaper at night.

He went on and on about how he liked to be on time for everything. The more he talked, the more I realized he was saying some racist shit. I picked up on it when he started saying things that began with, "most of y' all," "you people" and "coloreds."

Mrs. Lane grabbed my hand and squeezed it. I understood it was a squeeze of thanks and to pay him no attention.

We went on into the kitchen. The two multi-colored dogs came and sat around her while I prepared her breakfast. Mrs. Lane eyed those dogs in disgust. *Shoo! Shoo!* I assumed she said! Her stroke made it complicated to speak and for others to understand. Blowing fiercely, she positioned her hand under her chin in disappointment. They must have not obeyed.

I predicted she was too nice. My Grandma Louise would have Holy Ghost-filled with the spirit cursed Mr. Lane out if he were her husband. No way those nasty dogs would be in the house.

Once I finished cooking her scrambled eggs, cheese grits, bacon and toast, the dogs were up under me.

"Mr. Lane, can you please come get the dogs?" I yelled from the kitchen.

"Oh, they ain't gone do nothing," he said as he walked into the kitchen. "You colored people are scared of most animals."

Oh, no, he didn't. This time I could not keep my mouth closed.

"I am not scared of dogs; I just don't like mutts. Poor people have mutts because they can't afford dogs that have names, rich names like Saint Bernard, German Shepherd, Rottweiler, Yorkshire Terriers, Golden Retrievers; you know the dogs that come with papers."

I realized I was getting smart with my boss, but I didn't care. He would not disrespect me and keep saying lil' racist insults without me saying anything back to him.

"Papers!" Mr. Lane chuckled.

"Yes, papers." I folded my arms and gave him a slight neck roll. I was about to shit all over this man's ignorance. I unfolded my arms and positioned my hands inside the pockets of my red scrub jacket just in case they began doing more articulating than my mouth. "Dogs without AKC papers cannot be registered. I wouldn't own a dog I couldn't brag on," I continued. Mrs. Lane snorted before he could even respond.

Her drooping mouth and loss of speech didn't stop her from reacting to my 'leave me alone' humor. Looking at her trying to giggle warmed my heart. Many people in her condition wouldn't have dared cracked a laugh. The way she reacted made a big statement.

My second day moved quickly, because of Mrs. Lane's dialysis appointment. When we arrived back home, I prepared her lunch and, afterward, I left for the day.

However, before I left, Mrs. Lane grabbed my hand and kissed it with her soft lips. Her cold soft hand grabbing my sweating mushy hand was colorless just for a second. Mr. Lane looked disgusted, as his face turned red along with his Dumbo ears rising and sticking out from his head.

His entire body language changed as Mrs. Lane and I were frozen in time by the hand kiss. Mr. Lane's stare, tense body and teeth that bared in a snarl showed his alpha side. He is the pack leader of these mutts and the head of his home.

After she kissed my hand, she reached up out of her chair just enough to embrace me with a hug. She was grateful to have me. Just after one day, I felt her sincere appreciation for me.

I just wished her husband thought the same way. He ended that hug before we did by saying 'time to go'. I grasped that he hated observing his white wife kiss my black caregiving hands.

However, these black hands cleansed her pocketbook and ass, applied the cream to her bedsores, painted her toes, cooked her food, dressed her, pushed her wheelchair, made her bed, cleaned her shower, put her shoes on, combed her hair and brushed her teeth.

Nevertheless, it still was not good enough for a hug and kiss in the eyes of Mr. Lane. At that moment, I realized she wasn't problematic; he was. His hand by his side gestured me to leave as he said, "See you tomorrow."

Well, at least I still have a job.

I would get on my feet with this job. I could feel it. My single mother intuition improved more than my boyfriend-picking intuition. Either way, today was a good day with more income on the way. Eviction notes bothered my door monthly, embarrassing me by allowing my neighbors in my business, thus, enhancing my stress. This tactic made me, "hot and bothered." However, I continuously paid faithfully right before the so-called eviction court, but not this time; I'm two months behind. Planning my check for the next three weeks strained me, triggering another no-win situation. The thought of moving home was depressing. Mona needs her own little space, and I require my independence. One bedroom was adequate for us. Cable topped my want list, and lights topped the priority list. Bootleg cable burned my wallet, fifty bucks for borrowed time. For one week, I kickback and watch my favorite shows, then Boom! Cut off! Maybe this go-around, I would have enough left over after paying rent, utilities, etc. to get legit cable and have my hair done professionally. These bills too grown for me! Wishful thinking!

CHAPTER

FOUR

A few unbearable months went by working as Mrs. Lane's caregiver. Mr. Lane was undoubtedly an uninformed, bad-mannered, racist redneck.

"The man was ignorant, point blank, period."

My bond with Mrs. Lane grew strong. Most of the time she was mum, but her nods, facial expressions, sighs and body language expressed when she was happy, sad, frustrated, pissed off or tired.

We developed our own codes around the mutts and Mr. Lane. Every time he said something nasty, racist, prejudice or judgmental, she would apologize in her own little way by grabbing my hand and kissing it, patting my leg, hugging me, sighing or rolling her eyes. Mr. Lane's behavior embarrassed her, as he cursed more than rappers. His favorite words: son of a bitch, motherfucker and God damn it.

Mrs. Lane's earthly body entered the burning gates of hell each time he struck one of those words. When I saw the redness in her face, it was obvious that the stroke made Mrs. Lane's muscles too weak for speech.

The speech therapist diagnosed her with Dysarthria. She understood whatever she wanted to say and tried to say it. Mr. Lane and I didn't comprehend everything. Watching her fuss slurred or mumbled words at Mr. Lane for acting a damn fool was fucking hilarious.

I couldn't refrain from laughing my ass off in private. Mrs. Lane's mumbled words sounded familiar. She would say, "Ah-Choo," "Ugh," "Yummy," "Buzz," "Whew," "Duh," "Yuk -Yuk," "Whoa," "Ha-ha", she let out a bunch of sighs and her much-loved, "Shoo-Shoo!" Listening to her fuss sounded like, "Jibber Jabber."

Mr. Lane never understood her mumbled language. It never stopped his dominant side from telling her to back off. Mrs. Lane didn't stand a chance; he was trashy, and she was classy.

I learned at a young age while cleaning houses with Grandma Louise, that old money, wealthy, upper-class whites didn't speak to blacks as Mr. Lane does. If the upper-class whites did, they never voiced it around blacks. Only ignorant whites chattered that mess to blacks.

Mr. Lane probably grew up poor, uneducated and deep in the backwoods of the dirty south. He had little awareness of the world today.

Mrs. Lane made my job worthwhile due to her kind soul. She just married the wrong man twice. She had no children with her second husband, but Mr. Lane had children from his second wife. Mr. Lane's ex-wife died so this was a weird, second-chance, widowed love connection.

One day, around nap time, Mrs. Lane's friend, Margaret Benton, dropped by the residence with her husband, Mr. Leroy Benton. I answered the door, and they greeted me with a big burst of energy and relief of happiness because I was sitting with her. *Fake shit,* I thought, but I put on a smile and entertained the Benton's for the sake of my job.

Now Mrs. Benton was a well-kept woman. Her nails, toes and makeup were on point. Her blonde hair was flawless. The clothes she wore matched her personality.

I am the shit!

I am a rich bitch!

Two snaps and a head turn for the poor people in the back!

From what I gathered, they didn't like Mr. Lane, and anyone who didn't like him was a friend.

They communicated more with me than him. They asked me how old I was, what college I attended, how many babies I had.

Those questions kind of pissed me off. I needed no college degree to know it was a slick insult.

The Benton's visited for hours until my shift ended. Mrs. Benton occasionally skimmed around the house, with her nose elevated in the air. Mr. Lane always tried to showcase them ugly mutts, but not today. He knew Mrs. Benton's high-class society stuffy-ass wasn't the kind to engage with mutts.

Mr. Lane cursed and still allowed his underwear to show. He was real. Mr. Lane didn't give a damn about those uppity Benton's. I respected him for being himself no matter what.

I informed the couples it was five minutes past three. I was running over. Mrs. Benton sneakily offered to walk me outside.

As I opened my squeaky car door, she side-eye-winked at me, whispering we needed to chitchat real soon and requested my number. *This lady is weird as hell.* I gave it to her with suspicion. I figured it would be about more work, but I knew I couldn't work for anyone else because I had a baby.

Plus, she seemed too much of a snob for me to deal with. Mr. Lane had his ways, but he sure was not a snob. The way she strutted in the house with her Chanel bag, bending over kissing each cheek of Mrs. Lane as she rested in her wheelchair, gave it all away.

She called me before I got home. *That was quick,* I thought.

"Hello?" I answered the phone reluctantly.

"Uh, yes, is this Victoria? This is Mrs. Benton. We met at the Lane's house."

I peeped out my rearview mirror, not sure why. "Uh huh, I remember," I said.

"Can we meet at my house?"

What the hell? This was bizarre as hell. I'd just encountered her an hour before I got home, but my dumbass agreed to meet her anyway.

As I drove into her neighborhood, I shook my head. This was another loaded white person. *Where do they find this money? How do they make it so fast and at a young age? Maybe I should go back to college.*

I was already seventy thousand dollars in debt from student loans.

My GPS finally guided me to the house. It was huge. I thought it would be a clever idea to tag my daughter along, just in case this was another wealthy family. My institution was correct. Mona should see first-hand how we will live one day. My baby girl was entering her first of many mansions and not as a sitter.

We strolled up to her large, arched, glass doors with a dark brown frame, and I rang the doorbell.

I saw Mrs. Benton walking up to the front door through the glass. She opened the door and welcomed me as if we were friends and I was arriving to play a game of bridge.

"Come on in," she said in her country accent. "Awww. What a darling baby girl you have." She smirked as we entered her home. "What's your name, sweetheart?" She grabbed my baby's hand to play with her.

"Mona," I responded for her.

"Well hello, Mona," she said in a playful voice. "Put your purse down, dear, let me show you around."

We walked into the great room first, since it was nearest to the front door. I sighted the kitchen to the right of me and saw Mr. Benton standing by the stove looking like a suited-up pit bull. He had a football player body build with a tough coach attitude. His facial expression hadn't changed since I saw him last at the Lane's. Mrs. Benton's voice faded into the background as I continued to browse the room. The ceiling was so damn high.

Mr. Benton observed me checking out the beam extending across the ceiling.

"Thirty-foot beamed ceiling, one-and-only in Mississippi," he said.

"The two fireplaces were hand-carved," he continued.

Well damn, the coach does talk.

Bragging rights will end mutation.

As we entered the kitchen, my eyes bucked. Mrs. Benton spared no details when describing her Grand European Habersham top-notch kitchen. The kitchen was so spacious that she had two wide-spread islands that easily seated six people each. Ducked off another roomy breakfast area.

I used to fantasize about the *Fresh Prince of Bel-Air* mansion. *"Shiddddddddddddddd." Damn.* Will and Phil can have their house back.

Mr. and Mrs. Benton equally jumped at the opportunity to babble on. Combined voices sounded, gibberish. *Damn it, one at a time Benton's.* Once I entered their master bedroom, I could grasp the reason for the gibberish nonsense. "Holy cow!" The master suite resembled a luxury apartment in one of New York's high-rise buildings.

Their master suite had a fireplace, a private den with two white leather sofas turned conversational ways, and a his and her dressing room. I virtually collapsed the minute we entered her closet.

The closet mimicked an extremely large boutique store.

"Wardrobe room my ass!"

My apartment was tinier than her wardrobe room. No wire hangers were permitted. Mrs. Benton was a well-organized woman. All her clothing hung on wooden hangers, and her clothes were color coordinated.

The works!

The whole kit and caboodle!

You name it!

This wardrobe room was well-thought-out.

Wig's!!!!!!!!!!!!!!!

Lord, Mona and I slithered in, *"The Wig Boutique."*

I was flabbergasted!

Mrs. Benton's wig collection, *"uh no-expense-spared."*

Cross-questioning myself, like *"What year had white women wig life established."*

I mean, did we posse the same, wig sweeping wind Goddess?

I was dumbfounded.

Snob-life! Wig-life! You go, girl!

Mr. Benton wanted me to see his office, which also had a fireplace. His office looked like a mini library with oodles of books. Held by the manliest bookshelf I had ever laid hands on. *Yep, I had to touch it.* I was *that* black girl.

He had a lifeless deer head overhanging his desk. *"Ewwwwwwwwwwwwww."*

A portion of the wooden floor was concealed by an oversized cowhide rug with pinches of gold. Tasteful and, I bet, imported.

The gold on the cowhide was fire, but in my opinion, animals ought to be eaten, not used as office decor.

Masculine and sophisticated defined Mr. Benton's costly-looking office.

Mona weighed down on my hip. Thank God my little chocolate drop wasn't a crybaby. However, she grew irritated and jerked her girly yellow headband off her bald head. Normally, she wouldn't bother with it. I taught her early to keep it in place. Otherwise, people would continue mistaking her for a baby boy.

I was too afraid to sit Mona down in this over-the-top massive mansion. My baby could break something extremely rare or high-priced, costing both our lives.

It had been an hour. I wanted to know why Mrs. Benton called me, a stranger, over to their house in the evening, but they wanted me to see more. I was drained and ready to go home.

The next room pissed me off.

Who in the hell has a double oven in a laundry room? A Squanderer, that's who!

These people had too much damn money!

Mrs. Benton blew her own trumpet and smiled as if I was impressed. *Lady, you need your ass whipped, and your husband needs his beat for letting you do this stupid shit.*

"Wasteful!"

'Wasteful', damn near slid out my mouth, but I kept my mouth zipped.

"Mrs. Benton, you have a charming home, but I have got to take a seat. I've worked all day, and my daughter is heavy on my hip." We hadn't even made it upstairs. I had to say something, or else I would have been there all night.

Mrs. Benton led me to the extravagant over-decorated, great room. Immediately, I sat down. scooting back on the oversized leather sofa so I wouldn't slide off, while securing wiggly Mona tightly down in my lap. My new walking toddler was tempted to explore the ritzy room.

At last, Mona calmed down, realizing I wouldn't let her up. My toddler was worn out. Mrs. Benton sat quietly for the first time since meeting her, looking at us while Mr. Benton rummaged through numerous wooden cabinets before stumbling upon a reddish-brown leather photo album.

What have I gotten myself into? I thought.

Out of the blue, Mr. Benton rang a bell. I looked around cautiously. I didn't know what the hell was happening.

Of course. They had a maid; and, yes, she was black. Dammit. It never fails, and I wasn't surprised that her weaved tress was nappy and worn-out. Her edgeless hair somehow made a ponytail. The uniform was shabby, which made it appear sloppy and unkempt. Her dull black shoes had numerous scuff marks and were worn to shreds. It was evident the Benton's were compulsive shoppers, but frugal towards their domestic workers.

Every time I saw a black woman in a maid uniform and not a scrub set, I thought about their pride and how this was a tactic to make them less desirable.

Black women are always humiliated, and Mr. Benton is ringing a bell in 2005 to get his maid's attention. That only set the black woman back more. Just when I thought our race was being accepted, I was proven wrong again.

"Sallie," Mr. Benton called her. I immediately thought about my student loans with Sallie Mae. They stayed calling me for those defaulted student loans I never paid back. Hell, I thought maybe one of Sallie Mae's bill collectors had followed me to work or the Benton's knew Sallie Mae personally. Sallie's old-fashioned name was timeless. 'Black don't crack' did not apply. Good God was she wrinkled from the top of her forehead to her neck. I awkwardly waited for the Benton's to introduce us, sitting up high and mighty on this expensive ass shit. Hell, it never happened.

He asked for some freshly squeezed lemonade for all of us, but I was ready to go.

I asked them once again why they wanted to meet. Normally, I am a mild natured and patient, especially when I'm dealing with wealthy potential clients. I'm usually pleased when I need work, but I was sick of these two and this over-the-top ass mansion. The bell and Sallie made me uncomfortable. Seeing the Benton's penny-pinch Sallie was thoughtless, unsympathetic, insensitive and coldhearted of them; I was offended.

What in the hell do these people want with me? I'm young and stylish, and they will not turn me into a Sallie.

"Do you like to travel?" Mrs. Benton asked me.

"Yes, ma'am. I do," I said quickly, knowing damn well I didn't get out of Mississippi much, but I faked it. I'd already chosen a few states in my mind in case she asked about the places I'd travelled to so far.

"Well, where do you live currently?" she asked.

What the hell is this? Am I being interviewed? "An apartment complex in Ridgeland." I sounded frustrated on purpose.

"Does your mother live with you?"

"No, I have my place."

"So, have you ever been married?"

"No," I said. "I have never been married." The frustration was showing in the corner of my eyebrows and at the corner of my mouth.

"Does Mona's father support you and her?"

I was agitated at this point. "No." My leg began shaking. This lady was interrogating me. Next, she asked if I made a decent income to pay my bills and support Mona. Now, I ain't no damn fool; I know when to say "yes" and "no" to well-to-do people.

"We would love to help you and Mona out financially." She sipped from her small cup of tea. *"Help me but why not Sallie?"* I thought to myself.

I sat all the way up on the leather sofa.

"My husband and I have been in business for over forty years building and selling homes."

This lady spared no details when boasting about herself, her husband, her six kids, her business, her house, her vacations, her awards, her club memberships, her cars and her many, many accomplishments. Mrs. Benton was full of herself.

Frowned-up Sallie finally brought the lemonade. She was serving it as a waitress on a round silver platter. This lady never cracked a smile. Sallie had folded around her mouth. Bitterness and regret crisscross the wrinkles on her face. All the soul food in the world couldn't redeem her bitter soul.

I rubbed my smooth, youthful skin, telling myself, this would never be me.

Mrs. Benton yakked so long that the ice in the freshly squeezed lemonade melted.

Mr. Benton showed me the album he had been holding so long that his hands had turned ruddy. It was an album full of pictures of their six children, grandchildren and great-grandchildren. They had taken the time to label each picture with the names of who was in the picture, the place the picture was taken and the month, date and year it was taken.

"Hawaii, Christmas vacation with the children and grandchildren," was written on the very first page in the album.

I flipped through the album swiftly so I could go home. I was still puzzled about what they wanted with me or what kind of help they wanted to give me.

Let's cut the small talk and talk numbers; I am ready to go, I thought.

"My husband and I want to talk to you about Mrs. Lane."

"What do you mean?" I asked. I was confused and thrown off.

Mrs. Benton explained that Mrs. Lane planned to divorce her husband before she got sick. They'd married twice already and the first time, they were married right after high school.

"Why are you telling me this, Mrs. Benton? I'm just trying to work and take care of my child." I didn't understand why she gossiped with me about Mr. and Mrs. Lane's history together. I didn't care.

Mrs. Benton smiled and said, "How about you drive me to the country club tomorrow?"

Saturday? Oh hell no. That's my day off.

"Mrs. Benton, I'm sorry, I can't assist you." I picked Mona up off the sofa and walked towards the door.

"Sallie is off on Saturdays. I need you to drive me to the country club," she said frantically. It had gotten unbearable for her to park and then walk a long distance.

"I don't have a babysitter on Saturday."

"I want to help you, Victoria. I'll pay you $250.00 for the day."

Holding Mona on my hip, I slightly griped and asked her what time. "Should I wear scrubs or regular clothes?"

She faked a sneer. "Oh goodie, see you in the morning at 9:30 and you may wear whatever you please."

On the drive home, I telephoned my mom asking her to babysit Mona in the morning. I had to explain my part-time job. She cut me off, saying "Just bring me Victoria." It was late, almost 10:00 p.m. when I made it home.

CHAPTER

FIVE

*M*y alarm clock sounded at 7:00 a.m. This was a mistake, allowing my five-day routine to turn into a six-day routine.

I made it to the Benton's around 9:15 a.m. I tried to sit in my car until 9:30, but Mr. Benton saw me when he walked back up the driveway from getting the newspaper. I was stunned to see him dressed so early in the morning.

When I got to the door, I rang the doorbell even though I just saw Mr. Benton walk in.

"Come on in," he said. "Lela is still getting ready." That was his nickname for Mrs. Benton.

How cute.

I proceeded to the crammed great room and made myself at home. I bopped down on that lavish shit, crossed my thick legs and scrolled through a magazine. Without warning things got peculiar.

Mr. Benton unintentionally whiffed me with arousing cologne as he slumped beside me. I'm fond of good smelling men.

Stunting his fresh-out-the-cleaners khakis, button-down plaid shirt, brown belt and brown shoes to match. *"IGT!"* *"I see ya."*

His hair was naturally combed and placed strategically to overlay his bald spot. Then out of the blue, he held his hands out in front of me. I gave him a hostile look. *"Like get your wrinkled ass hands out my face."* I ogled his swagger but not like that.

"Do you notice the bugs on my hand, dear?"

I flinched backward in leaping a fighting stance. *"Flashback to some hood shit!"* Defending myself as if he had bugs on his hands, but as I eyeballed hesitantly, I realized there weren't any. Mr. Belton's fear-provoking bug-seeing ass shouldn't be around people.

"No, sir, I don't see any bugs," I said, distressed and mystified.

Mr. Benton grew unpleasantly aggressive and launched invisible bugs at me. *Flickering them like a booger.*

"I cringed and sidestepped at nonexistent bugs or boogers."

His voice intensified. "Got-damn it, Victoria you see 'em on my hand!" "Bugs!"

"They hand-picked me this morning when I retrieved that damn newspaper." He shouted.

"Hundreds of these got-damn bugs all over my motherfucking hand." He was getting rowdier.

Thinking, *"This is fucking ludicrous."* He cussed aloud; I cussed in my head.

Mrs. Benton hollered to him, panicking as she headed toward us from their downstairs master bedroom.

"CeCe, what's wrong, honey?" CeCe was Mr. Benton's nickname, I gathered.

"Lela, we have a fraud in the mansion."

Standing motionless, I clenched my mouth tighter, trying not to laugh my ass off in the Brenton's' face. However, I was tripping out in my head, saying to myself, *"These some ghetto ass nicknames for a white couple."*

WOW, 'a fraud, in the mansion'; this is some 'roll in aisles, fallout, lose your wig, cry-your-eyes-out kind of hilarious.

"Do you see all those bugs on his hand?" I asked.

"Yes, darling, I do." She snatched his hand, displaying so-called bugs to me. Even though I didn't see them, she motioned for me to say yes.

"Yep! I see them," I said.

Mr. Benton immediately transformed into a big wig once I agreed. He settled on the sofa, sophisticatedly crossing his legs, resembling a pacified dictator. I rolled my eyes on the sly at Mr.

Benton. Mrs. Benton gestured me to come closer to her. "Let me talk to you in the kitchen," she said. I thought you saw me roll my eyes.

I shadowed her like a misbehaved child. The second we entered the kitchen, she indicated Mr. Benton had early dementia and that she didn't want their children to know just yet.

"I'll keep your secret," I said.

In conclusion, we preceded to the country club, and it was jam-packed like Mrs. Benton stated. Once I drove up in the drop-off area, basically the front door, Mrs. Benton instructed me to return at 4:00 p.m.

Dang, that's a long meeting, I thought to myself.

Driving out the parking lot, my nerves were on edge. The steering wheel was dampened as my wet hands sweated from today's tension. I wanted to phone my mom or Grandma Louise desperately; however, I was paranoid they had listening devices in the truck, so I played it cool and turned the radio on to 97.7 to get my mind off the fact that I had to return to Mr. Benton.

Five days a week, I had to deal with Mr. Lane giving racial remarks, and now I had one day of pure craziness.

When I arrived in their neighborhood, I made a few blocks around the neighborhood. My favorite rapper, Young Jeezy, came on just when I was about to take it on in. 'Soul Survivor' made me burn another block.

As the beat dropped, I bopped my head and lifted one hand off the steering wheel, jigging as I rapped the song word for word.

The song faded out slowly as the radio host's voice came through the speakers to introduce a new song. That was my cue to face the bugs and Mr. Benton again.

I knew I had to take him to get something to eat, so I did, but that was an adventure of its own. Mr. Benton wanted to drive despite his current state, and I let him. I wish I hadn't. He burned rubber to Burger King, cursed people out in the drive-thru and insulted a Mexican worker at the window.

By the time we returned to the house, it was time for me to pick up Mrs. Benton, boy was I relieved.

When I arrived at the county club, she got in the truck and started talking before she even shut the door.

Dang, lady, unfasten your seatbelt and wrap it around your mouth.

On the way home, Mrs. Benton babbled that she and Mrs. Lane were members of this same organization; then at full blast, expressed how much she loved and missed doing things with her best friend. Once again, I wondered why Mrs. Benton shared details about her friendship with Mrs. Lane with me. These moments were so damn random.

When we made it home, I hurried her into the mental institution and hurled my goodbyes. Not once did she inquire about my day with Mr. Benton.

"Adios, Mrs. Benton," I said, being sarcastic but eager to leave.

"I'll need ya next Saturday at 10:00," she replied as I gathered my belongings to leap out the front door. I kept to my word.

"I can't work next Saturday, Mrs. Benton." She handed over my pay for the day.

"We will pay you extra," she whispered. "And you can bring your daughter."

Damn it. She got me again.

"Okay," I mumbled. "See you next Saturday." I was pathetic.

On the drive to my mom's house, I cussed myself out.

CHAPTER

SIX

*M*onday morning, I arrived at the Lanes' home, and I felt unperturbed. Mrs. Lane was paralyzed, but she wasn't envisioning bugs and cussing out Mexicans. She might be tongue-tied, but her mind wasn't tangled.

When I pulled up to their house, Mr. Lane was sitting on the porch in his chipped whitish rocking chair slurping black coffee with those hideous ass dogs alongside him. I guessed he was in a decent mood. He not only said, "Good morning," but he cross-examined my weekend. Whom my hands sweated for on my off days wasn't his business. Therefore, I didn't inform him the Benton's were now part of my livelihood.

"I had a breathtaking weekend," I said — no extra details.

Today was dialysis day; I walked through the door watching the clock. Punctual, I placed my purse on the table in the foyer. I hassled to their room to get Mrs. Lane ready. She was thrilled to see me, pleasant self. *Thank God.* She made my job trouble-free.

I decked her out in a fashionable purple jogging suit, did her makeup and fixed her breakfast while she finished her breakfast.

Guaranteeing to be punctual, Mr. Lane loaded her wheelchair into the trunk.

"Come on now, Mrs. Lane, we gotta go," I told her. She took her precious time eating the rest of her grits and eggs. I wasn't annoyed by this. I'd take my time too. On her last nibble, she slid her plate to the side and nodded her head, notifying me she was ready to ride.

I sat in the rear with Mrs. Lane while Mr. Lane drove us to the hospital. He was a break–the-speed-limit driver, but I knew I was safer. His driving skills were nothing like that fool from Saturday and the Lane's didn't chitchat as much as the Benton's, so I snoozed on the way to dialysis since it was forty minutes away in Jackson off Lakeland Drive. While we were out, we, at times, stopped to get lunch at Time-Out or Cafe 042, my favorite eating spot. They had the absolute best soul food. Mr. Lane was curiously generous. He bought my food and then invited me to sit at the table and eat lunch with them.

Grandma Louise instructed me to never sit at a table I am paid to clean. Zaka preached the same thing. Therefore, I declined.

As I watched them eat, I admired how proper Mrs. Lane's table manners still were. She situated her gray cloth napkin flawlessly across her purple pants in her lap. She waited until Mr. Lane was seated before she sunk her teeth into food. Mrs. Lane had a picture-perfect body posture. Observing her prompted me to tighten up and practice my stance.

Wednesday is hump day all around the world. However, it's my carousing day, the only day I get to let loose and partake in a turn-up. Last Ball was the spot-on Wednesdays, so I made sure my day at the Lane's never ran over.

Mr. Lane preferred grocery shopping on Wednesdays, right after Mrs. Lane's dialysis, if we went. That's when the new ads circulated. I knew what they wanted from the grocery store.

They ate the same food repeatedly. Frozen dinners, canned veggies and meals in a bag. Just add water, milk or ground beef. Even when they had a friend to bring to dinner, it was bland or some off the wall casserole. I had never heard of a chicken casserole with cornflakes on top as the breading.

Mr. Lane and Mrs. Lane had a grocery list, and I had mine. Mrs. Lane trailed around in the electric chair. She trailed behind Mr. Lane as he pushed the buggy. I was zooming down aisles as if I were a contestant on the *Supermarket Sweep* game show.

By the time the Lane's concluded their little shopping, I would've gotten Mr. Lane's credit card, swiped it, paid for the groceries and return it just to dilly-dally. My groceries for them were double bagged. I salvaged the additional bags to discard Mrs. Lane's wringing wet adulterated diapers.

When we made it home, the Lane's couldn't wait to watch me lug the bags in with exactly three trips to the car. I slipped numerous bags on my fingers to avoid making several trips. I put them up, got Mrs. Lane settled for the night and headed out for the day.

On Thursdays, I was always hungover and dog-tired from painting the town red, but I never publicized it. One Thursday, Mr. Lane traveled to the drugstore unaccompanied. I remained behind with Mrs. Lane. When he returned, he gifted me a toy teddy that sang alphabets for Mona. Under no circumstances had he ever gifted Mona or me anything.

When Friday rolled around, it didn't even seem like a five-day gig. Mr. Lane was oddly pleasant. Either he was bipolar or phony, but I'm not dim-witted, and I can't be hoodwinked. This man's unsympathetic racist habits towards "coloreds" as he says, didn't switch gears overnight. He can kick bricks with this tom-foolery.

On the other hand, Mr. Lane could be under the weather. Normally, wicked human beings develop a kind-heart without warning, before kicking the bucket.

Mr. Lane wrote my check out and handed it over as I stepped out the door.

"There's plenty where that came from," he chuckled, during which he winked his right eye. 'Identical' to Mrs. Benton's fabricated eye. That lady forced me to deceive her bug imaging husband! However, I don't have an inkling as to why Mr. Lane twinkled his prehistoric, brick slanging-ass eye at MOI.

Driving to the bank, my mind voyaged outer space; as my hands piloted the wheel, my foot clobbered the gas and my eyes navigated as I zoned out, thinking *these folks gone run me bat shit crazy!* At last, I made it to the bank to deposit my check. I should've glimpsed at it before I bolted out of Mr. Lane's house. He slipped-up and penned that bad boy for $1,000.00. My pay was $650.00 a week. I had to get out the long five o'clock bank line and give Mr. Lane a buzz.

"Hello," he answered promptly.

"Mr. Lane, hey, sorry to bother you after work hours. However, you miscalculated my wages and overpaid me."

"Oh, no worries, Victoria, it was intentional." I wished to monetarily express my appreciation for everything you do for my wife and me," he assured me. As I became emotional, Mr. Lane said, "Victoria, I've noticed you speak with a wide vocabulary; I mean you're very intelligent, but you go ahead and enjoy the rest of your evening," Mr. Lane told me as we hung-up.

Damn. I practically boohooed. My loudmouth called out to God thanking him for his favor. Mr. Lane's racially prejudice frozen-heart had been resurrected. "Glory be to God!" I shouted whimpering.

I emotionally returned to the bank line with thin-skin and cashed that 'Fat Check big-headedly. On my way home, I stopped and purchased groceries for Mona and Moi. Feeling Frenchy, I boiled spaghetti noodle, prepared my sauce and as it simmered, I added sautéed mushrooms; the fat-girl in me wanted deep-fried chicken wings. Cheers to Mr. Lane for allocating the funds to purchase my new Fry Daddy. Mona and I hadn't eaten a homecooked meal in months. My lack of income pointed me to 'Mama's House to Free-load'.

Every day I picked up Mona and headed to mama's house., Where I ate, swiped rolls of toilet paper, paper towels, garbage bags, dishwashing liquid and copped bars of soap, toothpaste plus mama did my laundry on a regular. So, tonight was a special treat. In the morning, I would return to the mental institution, the Benton's.

The Benton's handed me the green-light to bring Mona along since I did little labor. Even though Sabrina volunteered to babysit Mona, I decided at the last minute to decline Sabrina's offer. Instead, I accepted the Benton's offer, without giving prior notice to either of them. Tomorrow, my motivating force "Mona," would watch mama in action.

That morning, en route to the Benton's, I signed language Mona, giving her a thumbs-up. "To be a busybody in the mansion! A fine China, glass meddler in the mansion! And of course, a chocolate-drop, "Mona Menace," in the mansion!" I squirmed. She didn't understand a single word I spoke, but it pleasured me to be petty-minded.

I drove up, lifted Mona from her car seat and rang the rich sounding doorbell.

I'm trippin', I thought. *What the hell does a rich doorbell sound like anyway?*

Mr. Benton answered the door with blue shorts on and a plaid blue-and-white button-down shirt. Today we were "Siamese twins." I had on my blue fitted dress slacks and white button-down top. That was off-the-wall wild, plus he caught sight of it and spoke on it.

"Great minds think alike," he said. In my mind, I was thinking, *"no the flick of a wrist we don't."* He grabbed Mona's hand and played with her, mimicking a baby voice. This had to be a figment of my imagination. I couldn't believe a well-to-do white man was playing with Mona. It's been two consecutive days, where two white fellas have been overly polite. *Without a doubt its some hocus pocus going on. "My blackberry gullible ass has been bamboozled,"* I thought to myself, Lord, these white fellas done pulled the white sheets over my green eyes and ears. I bet my last dollar!!!!!! I'm the laughing stock, of the wealthy white folk, "Charitable Foundation."

Grandma Louise forewarned me about these domestic gigs, "It's full of twists and turns," she would say.

The first time I shadowed Grandma Louise at a gig, I was forbidden to play with toys that belonged to the white children. She was brought up during segregation. *However, Zaka said, it was frequently called Ghettoization, "Confined or Restricted to a Particular Area."* Grandma Louise did domestic gigs as a little girl shadowing her mother, Lucy. Playing with white children had been banned. Moreover, it was outlandish, bearing witness to innocent children of different races and ethnicity fraternizing.

Grandma Louise never evolved out of that era. In her eyes, everything was still labeled 'whites only' and 'coloreds only'.

Mr. Benton wandered into the great room, toting a bulky basket of toys. He then poured the toys out on the floor, spreading out puppets, dolls, medium size noisy teddy bears and other kiddie knick-knacks. Mona had the whole caboodle and more. We only lacked the prestigious Vintage Barbie, Mrs. Benton. She was still getting glammed-up. Mr. Benton was on his knees playing with Mona. He then slowly got up from the floor, sluggishly picking up Mona. I intervened by showing Mr. Benton that Mona walked. He then positioned her to walk with him. They both wobbled down a hall, eventually veering to the right as they entered a room. I quietly followed them, being the nosey overprotective mama I am.

We walked into what resembled a playroom for kids. That's when he sat Mona in a remote-controlled Ferrari car. I did not know of these gadgets for babies. Mr. Benton was controlling the thingamajig; he eventually steered her by the hand remote. Mona was giggling and drooling, having a blast cruising around the mansion. She was a boss baby. Then, the unthinkable happened without warning. Mr. Benton asked Mona if she saw bugs in the lines of the kitchen floor. Just when I thought we had a breakthrough, he proved me wrong.

"Mr. Benton, are you okay?" I asked nicely. I snatched Mona out of the remote-control car.

"This damn whatchamacallit car ran over all the bugs and killed them." His voice changed. "Do you see them?"

"I see them." That's how Mrs. Benton would have told me to answer, so I did. He skyrocketed up then shorty marched to his office. He brought back a white piece of paper from the printer. I didn't know what was going on.

"Can you get the bugs out the crack of the floor?" he demanded. "Be careful not to kill 'em." I prayed with my eyes open.

"Lord, why me? I am learning Lord, all money ain't good money," I prayed.

Straight bullshit! Early in the damn morning! Picking up invisible ass bugs in front of my daughter.

I furiously stooped down and collected fictitious bugs. Mr. Benton was bent over staring at me, *his bug gripping sucker.* He was resting the dearly departed on white printer paper. Mr. Benton got loud.

"Pick them up one by one!" he shouted. "Do you see any drops of blood on the white paper?" "No sir," I replied, as I slick rolled my eyes at him. I was cussing him out in my head!

Five days a week! "Oh, hell yeah Sallie went through it." Sallie, probably ain't that damn old. Dealing with this mindboggling spectacle daily, I'd be crumpled to eventually looking like a wrinkly old prune.

Not surprisingly, Mrs. Benton was all scalp, no hair; her husband's privileged circumstances. She undoubtedly planted the seed money for these so-called white women wigs. Together, they founded and funded this wig epidemic.

Finally, I can escape this mental institution by dropping Mrs. Benton off. So, I sprinted to my dusty black Chevy Impala to retrieve Mona's car seat. Out of breath, I zipped to Mrs. Benton's Range Rover and hurriedly buckled up Mona.

I was panicking as if Mr. Benton was coming with more bugs. Mrs. Benton nonchalantly pranced her way to the truck. However, I was buckled in with one hand on the steering wheel and my left hand on the gear shifter.

I was on the edge, sweating, full of anxiety. Once she shut the door, I immediately shifted in reverse and hard-pressed on the gas. Exiting the neighborhood, I released a lungful of air.

"It's peacetime."

Mrs. Benton informed me she wasn't going to the country club today. Instead, she was going to a hotel in Madison, off

Highway 463. I was familiar with Madison, but clueless on where the hotel was located. So, she directed and babbled on the entire way.

I was in high spirits driving into the hotel. That long-winded, mind-numbing lady bored me stiff, as she could talk the hind legs off a donkey. If she wasn't giving me directions, she was talking crazy shit about her husband. I tuned her out so much I didn't hear her ask me to escort her in.

But, "for $350.00 a day!" I would've lugged her back home to Barns Parie on my spine. I unbuckled sleeping Mona to escort Mrs. Benton into the lobby.

Mrs. Benton sashayed to the front desk and requested a room key. I was perplexed on why she demanded a room key. I thought maybe she had an engagement in a conference room at the hotel. Being silly, I followed her, hauling my baby on my hip.

I paid attention to her classy, skimpy clothes and realized she looked kind of seductive. She had an alluring shape, and her butt was firm in her white dress pants with a wide leg.

Those pants were figure-hugging.

She wore a button-down silk top, and three buttons at the top were left open. Anyone could sneak a peek at her perky breasts. I peeked at her perky tits, comparing them to my saggy tits. Her aged tits had my young ones beat. She clutched a white quilted leather Chanel purse trimmed in gold. The gold matched her gold, shiny belt accented with chains. My head slumped down and saw she had on Christian Louboutin red bottoms, but she couldn't walk that sturdy in them.

I recognized all the ritzy rags from the wealthy people's homes my Grandma Louise cleaned. They often offered Grandma Louise their unwanted clothes.

We stepped on the elevator, and it came to a halt on the seventh floor of the hotel, making a ding, as the silver stainless steel doors opened for us. Mrs. Benton glanced down at the room key to find the room number on the sleeve.

"Mmm. That's it," she said as she made a right off the elevator. We stopped at room 723. Before she could insert the key to unlock the door, a man unlocked it for her.

"Lela, you've arrived," he said. Before I made assumptions, I waited for her to introduce me to her son. "Baby." He grabbed her hand and softly embraced it as she introduced me. "Phill, this is the sweet young lady, Victoria I spoke to you about," Mrs. Benton said, in an erotic R-rated voice. I watched his fine, tall, dark-haired, suit and tie wearing-self before on television political campaign ads. However, it was none of my business. The Vintage Creeping Barbie had taste in men.

Rich and Powerful!

Her husband wasn't bad looking, but this Phill was more handsome. If I were a white woman, he would have most definitely been on my top ten hit-list. Phill had deep dimples engraved in both cheeks, a razor-sharp haircut and he smelled of fresh after-shave. His scent earned my vote, no matter what he was running for.

"Yes, this is my darling Victoria and her precious little girl, Mona," she replied.

Thinking, "Mrs. Benton knew how to kiss ass, I just hope she doesn't choke on that shit".

"Pleasure to meet you," he told me in a sexy, mildly deep, 'running for president' strong-debating kind of voice. I replied, "Pleasure's all mine." He shook my sweaty hand and quivered my soul. They are always wet when I'm nervous, but that wasn't the only thing wet.

Mrs. Benton's devious ways shouldn't have surprised me, but, switching her hip practically off while she walked Mona and me to the elevator, now that surprised me and entertained me. She tugged on my arm and stroked Mona's head as she conversed with me.

"When you have remained married as long as we have, sometimes you crave variety," she said. "Can I trust you to never mention a word of this to anyone?" Cheaters have no remorse until they are jammed up.

No wonder she dressed in her finest garments. The boldness of this two-timing Prima Donna was out-of-this-world disrespectful. This hotel was too close to home. Publicly cheating on her ill husband was risqué.

After today, I am not fucking with her hoe ass any more.

The woman in me was also tainted by a little jealousy.

Mrs. Benton was a real-life old Jezebel. I buckled my baby in, cranked the truck and just sat there. Then I realized she wasn't doing anything men haven't done. Men cheat and have mistresses all the time.

I drove up at the Benton's shamefaced and feeling part of a rummage-sale. Because I was used by Mrs. Benton and the guilt, I cared. Knowing her husband was receiving second hand Twat made me feel just as raunchy and undignified as her. I leaped out the vehicle level-headedly and forced myself to pull it together; then I walked around to unbuckle my daughter.

When I opened the door to the backseat, I saw a car pulled all the way up towards the basketball goal on the side of the house. It wasn't there that morning when I arrived, and it wasn't there when I left. I frantically walked into the house and searched for Mr. Benton. He wasn't in the great room, so I yelled for him. I didn't see him so, I kept searching around the house.

I just wanted Mr. Benton to know I had made it back.

As I proceeded back towards the great room, I heard loud clacking heels. I listened and pursued the clunking sound on the wooden floor. Holding my baby's hand, I corkscrewed around, stunned to see a woman. A young redhead towered over short Mr. Benton; she was much taller than him. Her long luscious legs were attention-grabbing. Rare treats came with a price only a trick could afford. Her green eyes overshadowed the scattered freckles on her face. She looked exotic.

I was eyeballing this beauty from head to toe, at a complete loss as to why; all this attractiveness was in this house alone, with Mr. Benton, then my phone rang. Mrs. Benton called my cell phone and dared to tell me she was done and that I could be on my way, but she wasn't the only one done.

We all got fucked that day.

I snatched the keys off the kitchen island in a hurry to leave the Benton's house of white lies. I proceeded to buckle my baby and myself up then burned rubber, zigzagging out of the neighborhood. I couldn't wait to scoop up the secondhand Prima Donna. Today, was my last day dealing with these people's insanity.

They are both freaks and hoes, I thought.

On the way, I stopped at a Burger Queen & Thing's and paid for a kid's meal for my daughter and a chicken sandwich combo for me. The drama made me crave something greasy and fatty. Normally, I am very professional by never being late. Today I didn't care; I fed my baby and dilly-dallied around in their truck.

We deserved it!

I drove up to the roundabout entryway of the hotel and saw Mrs. Benton standing at the front desk looking mangy as hell. So, I blew the horn to get her attention. Grandma Louise said hoes answer to the sound of horns. *Beep! Beep!* Here she comes, creeping out the front hotel door.

She slid in the truck grinning and trying to shoot the breeze. I made sure not to look in her direction, and I flew through intersections scurrying to get back to the house. On the drive home, she tried to give me marriage advice. She was convinced there was nothing wrong with double-dealing occasionally. Mrs. Benton lectured about how it's okay to basically have a side piece.

My friends and I call it having a side nigga. However, she's white so he wouldn't be a side nigga. At least Mrs. Benton didn't cheat downward. She spiced it up with a chiseled-body politician, and he was eye-catching for an older man!

When we pulled up in the garage, Mrs. Benton gripped my hand. She thanked me for not letting the cat out of the bag. *"But, she ain't keeping it in the bag!"* However, I gave her the cold shoulder; she didn't know if I had spilled the beans or not. Lucky for her, I don't tattletale, plus, I haven't had any damn time to call anyone and be a gossipmonger. This was a scorching-can't-touch-the-tea-cup kind of hot tea! Even though I had two secrets, Mrs. Benton's & Mr. Benton's, neither was my business; they owned this situation, not me. My motto, *"Less Mess, Less Stress."* As we walked into the house, she hollered for Mr. Benton.

She Ordered, Mr. Benton to pay me. He had my wages already sealed in an envelope, which I stuffed in my purse and rushed for the door. "I'll see you next Saturday, Victoria," Mrs. Benton yelled out from the great room.

I dropped the bomb on them, by giving my two-minute verbal notice, expressing to the Benton's that I needed to spend more quality-time with my daughter and that Saturday was the only day I had to spend with her.

Mrs. Benton increased the pay giving me a total of five hundred dollars for the day. I kindly declined, stating to her that my child comes first. Plus, my mind needed flushing-out from the Benton's immorality and deceitfulness. This shit was bigger than Mr. Benton flickering bugs like green boogers.

Like clockwork, the manipulating Mrs. Benton surfaced and, as predicted, she offered me double. I just shook my head and walked out.

She ran behind and begged me to come back into the house. I then rushed to put my baby in the car seat. I didn't care to hear anything else; my mind was telling me to leave. She blocked my hands from buckling my baby. The lady seemed desperate; blocking my hands grabbed my attention. She stared me in my eyes saying, "It's important."

I gazed at Mona, knowing damn well I would be making another mistake if I went back inside, but Mrs. Benton baited me in. This isn't the life I expected to portray in front of my daughter no matter her age.

Dead on my feet, tired of the Benton's, I entered through the same white garage door I swore, by no means, to see again. I took a seat once again in the great room.

Mrs. Benton started by saying she wanted to make sure I could be trusted.

Really? I thought. *Trusted?* Of all the words she could've used, trust should have been the last one.

She looked at Mr. Benton with a concerned look on her face. "Go get the contract," she said to him.

Mr. Benton hightailed it to his luxury road-kill office and brought back a manila envelope with a few pages of paper attached to it with a paperclip. It was a confidentiality agreement. Basically, they didn't want me to disclose anything I had witnessed and heard during the entire time they employed me.

"I'm ah Eavesdropper, not a Stoolpigeon!"

"Why do I have to sign this now?" I wasn't coming back to work for them anymore, not after this.

"I need your signature to continue this conversation with you, dear."

Mr. Benton put on his masculine, demanding voice. "Have you disclosed anything about us to your friends or family?"

"No," I told him. I wasn't raised up to be the town's blabbermouth.

"Plus, nobody would even believe this shit."

Even though it's the Godly truth, I would've been labeled as a *"big blackberry fabricator."* I also didn't wish for my friends and family to know these well-to-do snowflakes had me on my knees picking up invisible bugs. It's easy to laugh and tell my people he flickered bugs like boogers, but it's not comical to tell my people I picked-up them boogers.

I was already afraid that Zaka had front-row seats in heaven and viewed me on the big-screen kissing these people's ass for a dollar. I bet he was furious. If that didn't get Zaka booted out of heaven, I bet me re-entering their house and signing this agreement would.

I handed back the agreement signed and dated. They both scrutinized it and questioned me once again, double-checking to ensure I hadn't blown the whistle on them. Then they elaborated on everything that had taken place each Saturday.

Mrs. Benton was a notorious talker, and I didn't have it this evening.

"What do you have to talk to me about? I am ready to go home." I was fed up.

The redhead must've sucked Mr. Benton up. He finally grew balls by intervening and telling his dominant wife to cut to the chase. I felt this way because he never spoke to her in that aggressive manner.

Mrs. Benton strutted the pants and the panties. That's when she explained that she hadn't cheated on her husband. She only told me to keep her secret to see if I would. My face dropped down in my hands as if I had started a prayer. They both had an agreement and understanding. It's not cheating when you don't lie and hide extramarital affairs from your spouse. Mrs. Benton's then explained that she and her husband were swingers.

What the fuck is a swinger?

She confided in me they swap spouses or have casual sex with other people. *"Whaaat? I knew it! I knew it! I always knew they were freaky."*

Mrs. Benton claimed swinging improved her husband's dementia and added more excitement to their marriage. With her legs crossed, she said they had been swingers most of their marriage but with couples their age. However, Mr. Benton's dementia grew so detrimental that Nursing Home placement became her only option; then she realized Mr. Benton hadn't forgotten how to engage in sex.

"Ahem," she sounded as she cleared her throat as if she was embarrassed to say, "He stayed on hard three times more than the men his own age." She went on saying, "Most men Mr. Benton's age had developed erectile dysfunction."

Mr. Benton glanced at me like, "Yeah I still got that juice."

I eyeballed them both like, "Man Ole Man I'm glad my black ass came back in."

However, his stamina became too much for Mrs. Benton to bear and for couples around their age, so they found a younger couple. That's when Mr. Benton started getting better. His speech drastically improved, along with his memory.

He just wanted, "A pass to get unlimited ass."

Mrs. Benton said the young nameless redhead, as they continued referring to her, has made Mr. Benton feel youthful, desired and more important; she kept up with his high sex drive. Imaging short, bug seeing, none-driving Mr. Benton having a high sex drive. *"EWW!"*

She goes on by saying, now she only had to deal with him seeing invisible bugs.

They promised one another that the nursing home facility would be the last result. Mr. Benton stated that he sought after me to help them.

To help them. Help them do what? Swing and pick up invisible bugs? Mr. Benton walked around the great room, pacing the floor with his whiskey glass in one hand, spinning the ice cubes around in his whiskey. His diamond pinky ring and gold bracelet gave him a huge ego today.

Finally, the man of the house slammed the glass down on the black-and-cream-colored marble tabletop.

Mr. Benton's face was pleading. "Victoria, we need something else." He paused. "We need your help with Cary and Tommie." At last, my long-standing question was answered.

The Benton's didn't need additional help on the weekends, just as I suspected.

Gee-wiz, "these people are treacherous!" Thank God my baby had been fallen asleep and was stretched out on the fabric sofa under the high-rise glass window in another seating area in the great room. This wasn't a conversation anyone should hear regardless of age. Because, when Mrs. Benton spilled the tea, *my cup runneth over*. Grandma Louise always recited this verse growing up. I misinterpreted this meaning when she quoted this scripture:

Psalms 23:5 "Thou preparest a table before me in the presence of mine enemies: thou anointest my head with oil; my cup runneth over."

The Benton's switched the gears to the Lane's at full speed.

At first, I was confused when Mrs. Benton referred to the Lane's as Cary and Tommie because I hadn't known first names. I asked both Benton's, "Who are Cary and Tommie?" I didn't give them time to answer me. "Is that the redhead and the man Phill from the hotel?"

"Heavens, no. Cary isn't the redhead," Mr. Benton answered quickly. He even chuckled as if I had humiliated him.

"Cary and Tommie are the Lane's," Mrs. Benton said, as she rolled her eyes at me like *"DUH!"* "Oh yeah," looking dimwitted because my check said, "Tommie Lane and Cary Lane," every week.

Mrs. Benton continued saying that Mr. and Mrs. Lane had been married twice as if I didn't know that. *"DUH!"* rolling my eyes this time. Apparently, Mr. Lane abused Mrs. Lane when they were younger. Mrs. Lane remarried after she and Mr. Lane divorced the first time.

Mrs. Lane's second husband was a very affluent businessman here in Jackson. They were married well over forty years when he perished, which left her very well off.

Mrs. Benton went on saying that Mr. Lane read of his death in the *Clarion-Ledger* and that's when he contacted her. The Benton's instantaneously became suspicious of Mr. Lane's motives when the rumormonger spread. "AHEM," clearing her throat, while twirling her necklace around her neck as she's feeling it's un-ladylike to say such rumored things about a friend.

The word on the street was;

Cary's husband's corpse wasn't even barebone when Tommie started boning her

Mrs. Lane kept hush-hush about her rekindled relationship with Mr. Lane. The Benton's alleged he spell-bounded and isolated her. Mrs. Benton hated to admit it, but Mr. Lane had been her first love and more than likely, her first everything.

"Love is blind because Cary never arranged a meeting with her attorney to draw up a prenup," Mrs. Benton said. I perked up when I heard prenup. I hated to sound dum-dum. However, I didn't understand what she meant by prenup at first.

"It's a law-abiding agreement that would've protected her money and property in case they divorced again," Mrs. Benton explained. "Tommie would have only been entitled to what he came into the marriage with. Everyone was surprised; she remarried him without a prenup."

The Benton's did not understand why she'd moved and sold her garden home the Benton's had built for her. The Benton's built and sold homes for a living, so it was understandable. Mrs. Benton was perturbed that Mrs. Lane didn't contact her when she and Mr. Lane purchased their new home together. That's like having a friend that sells Jordan's, but you buy them from the mall instead. Well, maybe not the same.

Mr. Benton turned reddish like the hair of his green-eyed, freckled-face afternoon snack. Angrily, he said, "Mr. Lane has been spending her money like he earned it."

Staring at him like, *"ANNNDDDDDDD so what? This isn't my misfortune."* He got hot and bothered telling me about the new cars, a big RV, motorcycles and an in-ground pool that Mr. Lane purchased.

Mr. Lane's, "Cup-Bank Account Runneth Over," with Mrs. Lane's money.

It, infuriated Mr. Benton watching his new enemy indulge in the fruits of another man's labor.

Shortly after, in a very arrogant approach, Mrs. Benton re-entered the conversation and explained how the Lane's had gone on a couples' trip to Canada. Then suddenly, Mrs. Lane had a stroke.

Suspiciously, Mrs. Benton said, "Cary confided in me days before us vacationing saying that she was sick and tired of Tommie's bull-crap."

Thinking to myself, *"Just say bullshit."*

Mrs. Benton went on saying, "Cary told me this would definitely be their last couples' trip, because she was divorcing Tommie as soon as they came back."

Thinking to myself,

"Damn... it was her last couples' trip; Mr. Lane immobilized the hell out of her."

Mrs. Benton said, "The divorce never happened, and now he has control of all her money." "That he didn't earn," Mr. Benton added his two cents. Even though this was a serious conversation, I was on pins and needles waiting for Mr. Benton to see bugs again, but it didn't happen. I guess the redhead cured him for the day.

I guess Mrs. Benton couldn't let this shit go, because she had more to tell me. She reminded me that Mrs. Lane had no children and only one sister who lived in Kent, Indiana.

"We are her family," Mrs. Benton said, as she picked up a glass cup off the black marble table that sat next to the recliner. The smell of vodka mixed with cranberry juice seeped from her cup. "She is like my sister; I have known her since we were in college."

Right then and there, I knew the Benton's only motive was to inform me of who Mr. Lane was. They didn't need me to drive or even work for them as I had been.

They just needed me to help obtain evidence that Mr. Lane was abusing his wife. I wanted to know how else he had been abusing her, besides her tailbone being covered with bedsores from being wet for hours after I leave.

I witnessed no physical abuse. So, I asked, and I received my answer. The Benton's felt like he was poisoning her and that's why she had a stroke.

They assumed Mr. Lane had learned or possible heard of her plans to divorce him. Before her taking ill, he would intimidate her into doing whatever he wanted her to do. Sometimes, she would have a bruised arm, leg, back or butt.

Mr. Lane was cautious and cunning, never to strike her face or visible parts of her body. The Benton's felt that if it could be corroborated, that he was an unsuitable caregiver, then Mrs. Lane would be removed from his care; therefore, the Benton's would pay me extra to assist them in gathering evidence to file charges and acquire Mrs. Lane.

Now it's my turn to be livid! Just like Mr. Benton was at Mr. Lane. I was overheated, mad as a human furnace on the inside. If I didn't bank on my good name as a caregiver, I would've tongue-lashed these rich pricks to the fiery gates of hell.

These hypocrites made me sign my life away, to safeguard the fuckery within this mental institution, by ensuring I stayed tight-lipped about their privacy.

"WOW, the pot calling the kettle black some nerve."

One hundred dollars a week to be a *B.U.S "Black Underpaid Snitch."*

The Benton's, I myself and sleeping Mona all sat in silence as the great room now had its much, needed moment of silence.

Mrs. Benton got up. She said her drink was getting low, so she headed toward the kitchen. "Won't ya come to help me, darling?" Mrs. Benton motioned for me to follow her.

I'm not stupid. I knew she was up to something. It doesn't take two people to mix a drink. Hell, it was just vodka and cranberry juice.

When we made it to the kitchen, Mrs. Benton pulled me aside.

"You can't let Mr. Lane find out," she said in a sneaky, lowdown, devilish voice. "Here is your first payment. Plus, you can keep all of today's pay." She said that as if I hadn't earned it. This lady had a lot of self-assurance — some things money can't buy. I can't be brought for an extra hundred a week. The Benton's probably wanted guardianship of Mrs. Lane, to dominate her money like Mr. Lane. Gluttonous people stay hungry for bread; their appetite can't be satisfied.

Mrs. Benton rested her hand on my shoulder, looking me in my eyes saying, "If you agree, I'll pay you cash every Friday, when you give me my report," she continued to say.

I couldn't take her seriously, "her damn wig was crooked."

Report!? It's time to go before I snap out and pop that crooked ass blonde wig off her scalp. Even though I am violating every code by saying yes, if I refused, I'd spend the night over here as Mrs. Benton and I would never see eye to eye. Therefore, I will join the game and pretend to be her B.U.S "Black Underpaid Snitch." I will go with it.

I agreed to the Benton's terms. Might as well keep playing along and get paid.

When we re-entered the great room, Mrs. Benton enthusiastically shared the news with her husband. They both grinned like devious devils, saying I was now like family. My definition of family means we are blood-related, but we are loyal to each and we have one another's back. Real family don't put you in compromising situations.

In my eyes, this was more of a set-up or a plan of greed. I knew Mr. Benton's rock-hard male ego had been touched.

Family my ass! Family don't give you a couple of hundred dollars a week and make you sign an agreement not to snitch on them, and then pay you money to snitch. Family would have given me one vehicle that they don't drive.

The word family was my exit word to leave. Again, I said my goodbyes, grabbed my sleeping baby and all our belongings. All that "we want to help you and your daughter out financially" was bait. They'd cat-fished me.

They then walked me to the door; every step on their polished wood floors reminded me of the terrible decisions I made.

However, on the upside of things, I could almost pay my rent with one week's pay. Paying daycare and still having a little left over would be awesome. Zaka always told me, "Stay down till you come up." I was slowly coming up.

This could mean a hundred and seventy dollar sew-in plus bundles for me. I was still young and sexy. The struggle of single motherhood limited my funds. In high school, they use to call me Laura Winslow from the TV show *Family Matters.* These days I favored Harriette Winslow, the mother by the head only.

My upkeep of myself had been neglected, but I was still young and sexy. I missed getting my nails, toes, eyebrows and lashes done. Looking back at the old me and staring in long mirrors at the new me depressed me. I labored harder than most couples, but as one person to pay bills and stay afloat.

All the extra money I had made from the Benton's had me back on track with all my bills, so I let this B.U.S. girl act ride for a couple of months, but I also reported false information to the Benton's, and they paid me as agreed every Friday.

CHAPTER

SEVEN

On Thursday, July 18, 2007, my life changed forever. Mr. Lane was extra whacky that day. We rode around viewing homes for sale, and he purchased my lunch. Then enquired about Mona calling her by her first name and not "your baby" or "that baby."

As we peeped out one rich neighborhood after another, we stopped at a breathtakingly gorgeous, home with a huge lot.

"You'll never possess a home like this, not with what I pay you," Mr. Lane said as he chuckled. When we pulled into the driveway, my spirit was suddenly saddened. I hated to admit it, but Mr. Lane was spot-on. I could never possess a home like the Lane's and the Benton's. I barely possessed my tiny one-bedroom

apartment. With both job, I only made a little under seven hundred dollars weekly.

This reminded me of my big cousin, Zaka. On our many visits to the library, Zaka had read and explained how the housing projects had been developed.

Many whites during the 20th century believed having blacks in a white neighbour-hood would bring down property value. The United States began making low–interest mortgages available to families through the Federal Housing Administration.

Black families legally could have these loans, yet many had been denied due to the many black neighbourhoods being called "in decline." Zaka told me they always could keep black families from owning houses. New laws eventually forced banks to stop denying us home loans.

If a black family wanted to purchase a home in a declining area, the application was denied. The loans didn't cover areas marked as declined.

The whites then started moving to the suburbs, building and developing prominent white communities. They were encouraged and provided with loans to move.

On top of being denied loans, Zaka had told me the government uprooted black families. Development of highways through black neighbourhoods pushed the families out and to *"The Projects"*, barely receiving anything for housing.

Zaka, told me this is how the "The Projects" developed. Our government built and funded "The Projects" in a plot to intentionally hold blacks back from owning a piece of America. Homeownership was and will forever be "The American Dream", especially mine.

Furthermore, Zaka always made me aware of how the world worked so I would do better. Homeownership was my main goal, and that will never change. That's why I reported as a good ole girl to the she-devil each, week making an extra one hundred dollars, so really, the joke was on him this time, even though I re-counted the Benton's bull-crap each week.

"Dang I now cuss like classy Mrs. Benton, saying Bull-crap instead of bullshit."

They still had arrangements to move Mrs. Lane out of the home with Mr. Lane. They also promised to pay me double once they retrieved guardianship, but still, I trusted none of them.

Every day, I must deal with being black and have white people making me feel uncomfortable for being black. I must work double, be a "B.U.S," and play nice to make ends meet.

The Benton's wanted me to help them save Mrs. Lane, but who would save me if they threw me under the bus? Nobody would ever believe a word I said about this entire situation.

I searched for another private care sitting job. Hell, I thought I might need to get out of the caregiving field altogether. Tax-free money was so good. I just hated that I had to be in so much mess to get it. I should have completed college and had a baby after I was married.

Lord knows I should have listened to my mama and kept my legs closed. If I would have waited, went to college and began a career before a baby, I wouldn't have been dancing with the devil just to make cheddar, but the bills had to be paid.

I cheesed Mr. Lane's insults off and ignored him while he kept driving and yakking. I was getting paid to ride and view homes. When we returned to the house, I settled Mrs. Lane in for the night and gestured to Mr. Lane to let him know I was leaving. As I headed toward the front door, he decided he would walk me to my car.

"I don't pay you enough to purchase a home." Mr. Lane repeated what he said from earlier. "I know you want a new place for you and Mona. Mrs. Lane has more than enough, old and new money from her money-making second husband." He kissed his pale spotted fingertips and tossed them away something like an Italian hand gesture. As he continued to gloat about money and told me, "My dear 'little' wife also has a very profitable life insurance policy."

I thought to myself, *yeah, she is small. The poor lady barely ate anything. Even though she had survived the stroke, it made eating, chewing and swallowing food damn near impossible.*

"I often whipped -up boost shakes by adding ice cream, whole bananas, yogurt and anything else that was fattening on hand. I didn't change a lot of Mrs. Lane's adulterated diapers. So, I knew she had some nourishment that remained on her." The conversation carried on between Mr. Lane and me.

"Okay? What does that mean to me?" I nonchalantly asked him.

"It could mean a lot to you if you let it. If you help me, I will help you get a home."

Aww Damn, "The Help Word."

My heart began thumping rapidly. I desired a lovely home for my baby and me so badly.

"What do I need to do?" I pretended I didn't care. It was a part of my reverse psychology tactic. If I acted laidback about purchasing a new home, then he wouldn't sense I was desperate.

The biggest blooper I made with the Benton's was being eager for a dollar and childlike. The Benton's preyed on my immature mind. Therefore, they took me fast. This is a grown woman's game; its time I boss up and play the game how it's supposed to be played.

Mr. Lane then altered the conversation and asked me what I had done with that, as he called it, "Lil thousand -dollar check." I told him, "I lacked food at my apartment, so I made groceries and purchased a Fry Daddy," as if it had any merit to this present conversation.

Just when I thought we made headway, Mr. Lane, while doing his petty redneck chuckle, says, "I am on cloud nine Victoria, you can snatch my tongue-out and render me speechless, that you didn't walk off with any of my food for you and that little hungry baby."

He attacked my dignity even more by saying,

"The colored's pilfered food and anything else they could get their hands on."

"Glad you're not a pilfer Victoria," he said, chuckling once again.

I didn't find this shit funny! And I almost let this comment roll, considering he was just discussing money. However, this time, I would not be zip-mouthed. I told that chuckling, Dumbo-eared Mr. Lane, as I pronounced every word to the T, while rolling my neck and speaking with my hands,

"I don't have the taste buds for bland foods. Nor, do I gobble-up meatless casseroles with cornflakes for its toppings. Neither do I devour, just add water and canned chicken breast foods daily. I am not on a diet! Instead, I am in love with soul food and all things fried."

Mr. Lane immediately switches his tone and says,

"I didn't mean to offend you, Victoria and I apologize, I was just kidding around. I didn't mean any harm; and I know you wouldn't make off with, nothing of mine," he says sounding sincere.

Mr. Lane apologized in the nick of time. Because I was about to knock his head off by telling him, I don't eat the cooking of women with skinny ass arms, that stay-at-home and live at the gym-part-time. *Women with skinny arms don't fry chicken; they fry hair.*

If her arm ain't hefty like mine, then guess what: "The Bitch Can't Cook!" But I muted my tongue and humbled myself. Plus, his apology, well let's just say "that's a first." I 'm so over the prejudice, stereotyping, racist remarks of Mr. Lane.

I was eager to know what he needed my "Help" with. Before I put my foot in my mouth, Mr. Lane apologized again, as he told me how I could help him.

He said, in a low polished, pitiless way, "If you help me get her to heaven a little faster, I will compensate you a check for fifty thousand dollars." My heart plummeted into my stomach and, before I knew it, I vomited on his shoe.

"Shit!" he yelled. He sprinted over to the grass to wipe his shoes off.

Mr. Lane's elongated, redneck face turned bloodshot red as he continued to curse, mimicking a real Italian. I glanced around like the drama queen I am. Hell, I felt like I had taken a portal ride to New York. His demeanor changed quickly.

He habitually utilized the word motherfucker. In this instant, I was many motherfuckers. At this moment, my body immobilized. I was stiffened. All I could do was think about what a wicked monster Mr. Lane really was.

I felt horrible for puking on his old man tennis shoe, but when I heard the money he was proposing, I couldn't aid myself. I never had a great deal of Benjamin's. Hell, I didn't know anyone that was loaded with Benji's like that, but the well-off white folks I labored for.

Why would anyone want to murder someone they married twice? I thought.

The shady, freaky Benton's were factual this entire time. He wanted sweet, naïve, gullible Mrs. Lane dead, but I was afraid to confront him.

He stepped out from the grass, walked towards the cemented driveway and stood in front of me. I stood there emotionless and dumbfounded.

He leaned in a little closer so I could absorb his soft-spoken firm words. "If you speak one word of this to anyone, I'm gonna dangle you like they used to do the Blacks."

Damn! Damn! Damn!

Now my dreams might be coming to pass in an awful, life-threatening way. Reminiscing, about what Zaka once told me about old-school white people. "If a white man kills another white man, you know a black life really has no value," he told me.

I slowly opened the door to my Chevy Impala and jumped in. He stood there staring at me unsympathetic. As I wiggled the keys in the ignition, I peeked up at him through the front window. He held one arm up displaying a hanging gesture. I mashed on the gas pedal and backed up so recklessly that I virtually hit the mailbox trying to make a speedy right turn out the driveway.

When I returned home, I prayed and prayed. I didn't wish to go back, but I had no other income. Rent was coming up, and I needed that check. I could barely put gas in my car at the end of the week because I was waiting to get paid every Friday.

CHAPTER

EIGHT

When the sun arose, I was a saddened. I didn't want to return to the Lane's, but I had no other alternatives. I took a lengthier route to Mr. Lane's that morning and purposely drove slower than normal. I had a lot on my mind; private sitting was supposed to have been enjoyable. Taking care of aging adults should have been peaceful for my clients and me; instead, my life was in shambles. As I turned into the Lane's driveway, my hands were clammy, as I became extra faint-hearted.

I strolled up to the brick steps and rang the doorbell. Mr. Lane opened the door before the doorbell even chimed. He didn't say, "Good morning dog, rat, cat or colored girl." He immediately said, "Come with me right now." I followed him to his office, cautiously.

I was frantic and timid, *"Lord please allow me to cast my slanted-eyes on Mona again,"* I said in my head. I took a long deep breath, relieved that he handed me a check. Mr. Lane was one hundred percent old-school. Therefore, he only understood one system, "pay-as-you-work." Not beforehand, nor this early in the morning. Something was up.

As I reached for my check, I felt sweat collecting in my hands; the tip of the check was already moist, and it was hardly in my hands. My eyeballs expanded practically rupturing out of its lids. The check was written to; Victoria Lewis for fifty thousand dollars. There it was in black and white, signed and dated by Mr. Tommie Lane.

"Mr. Lane, this is not correct. You only owe me six hundred and fifty dollars."

"I paid you precisely what I told you; I'm a man of my word."

"You can cash it today. If you cash it, we have an agreement."

"No, sir!" I commanded. "I cannot do that!"

"Why is it that you wrote me a check for one thousand dollars for me to basically buy groceries, but now you're writing me a check for fifty thousand dollars to buy me a home, this just doesn't make any sense to me," I said to Mr. Lane.

"Victoria you get what you pay for, I can pay you an extra three hundred and fifty dollars a week totaling, a weekly thousand dollar check, which means you and Mona will have groceries temporarily to eat or I can put you in a position to permanently eat.

The better position you're in, means, the better position I will be in. See Victoria money would be useless to me if I am in prison. Do you understand I am your meal ticket to a better life and you're my meal ticket to a prison-free life? I need you, and you need me Victoria," Mr. Lane preached to me with confidence.

I understood his reasoning, a lot better. For paying me, such a life changing amount of cash, the Benton's were stingy, penny-pinching me a buck a week, to be a B.U.S.

Mrs. Lane's blood is on their hands; they should have been overgenerous to MOI. Mrs. Benton should have been a wasteful-spendthrift on her best friend's life, just as she had been with those double-ovens in her laundry room. Then I would have allied with them to save Mrs. Lane's life instead of being in cahoots with Mr. Lane to take her life.

Per se Mr. Lane, *"you get what you pay for."*

This is nothing more than just a huge kickback to shut the hell up and mind my own damn business. Whether he pays me or not, she will still be peacefully put to sleep. I signed a written agreement with the Benton's not to disclose anything about their private life and now I am doing the same thing with Mr. Lane, except it's a verbal agreement.

I said, "Okay, Mr. Lane what exactly are you requiring of me?"

"Just vouch for me that she was terminally ill. Victoria if you have my back, I will have your back. Nothing will be hands-on, just simply back me by saying, she had taken sick just a few weeks back. Don't worry yourself; it won't be an overnight death, he said, callously."

"It'll be slow. My strategy is to compensate you beforehand, making it look as if I was very gracious to our, *"Black Ma'Sitter."*

Money overpowered my integrity, and fifty thousand dollars was in my hand. Now, Mr. Lane was evil as fuck for trying to murder his wife, but at least he wasn't leaving me out, and I was cashing out profitably; furthermore, he didn't make me sign anything like the Benton's.

I felt bad for Mrs. Lane, but I felt damn good for myself.

I had been on the edge since I had begun working for the Lane's and the Benton's. Both couples had spun me into someone I never knew existed inside of me. I was once just a single mother out here hustling and bustling for my daughter, but each dollar I earned from the Lane's and the Benton's came with a price.

As the day went on, I thought about going to the police and reporting Mr. Lane, but I knew no one would ever take the word of a black sitter. Moreover, Mr. Lane had the bread that could have me blackballed and poor or bumped off and dead in Mississippi.

Furthermore, if I mentioned it to the Benton's, they would probably flip-flop on my blackberry ass too. I had only one option, and that was to *"Pocket the Benjamin's baby,"* I said with excitement, rolling my neck and snapping my finger.

Zaka never schooled me on what to do if something like this ever transpired.

Maybe it had never happened to another black sitter. I could be the first and only sitter offered money to watch someone slowly knock-off their wife. What in the hell was I thinking? These big-bank snowflakes done twisted me into a money-hungry, swayable materialistic villain.

Mr. Lane provided me the address of the bank where he instructed me to cash the check. He also handed me a yellow sticky-note. Written on it was the name of the Truss-bark Bank Manager for me to ask for. Her name was Karen Johnson, and she would be expecting me.

I didn't put on my skates and skate to the bank, which should have been expected, because so many thoughts were jammed-up in my mind.

What if this is a setup? What if he called the bank back and told them I held him up with a gun and made him call so I could cash that check then run off to Mexico?

I pulled over on the side of the road and sat there for almost thirty minutes. While I sat there, Mr. Lane called and asked why I had been just sitting on the side of the road. I quickly flipped up my sun visor and gazed around with my cellphone glued to my ear.

First, he approaches me to slaughter his wife, then he threatens to lynch me and now he's trailing me.

This is not what Zaka meant when he was encouraging me to be a boss.

As I gripped my phone, thrown-off and emotionally tapped-out, Mr. Lane demanded I catch the bank before it closed.

Before I hung up, he jogged my memory of a previous threat by angrily saying,

"You better keep your motherfucking fly zipped or I'll go fly-fishing!"

"Stringing your ass up like a largemouth black bass!"

I hung the phone up smoothly and kindly. I had no sarcastic comebacks, realizing this ain't no joke. Mr. Lane ain't playing like the Benton's. This was real and playtime was over.

As I pulled into the bank, I had to perk my punk ass up. However, I was still in the parking lot watching for the cops, but as I opened my door, I realized there wasn't a cop in sight. I unhooked my seatbelt thinking about fly-fishing and decided I better cheerfully strut my largemouth, black bass ass, right on in that bank. Mr. Lane had whipped my mind right back into shape by activating my bipolar spirit with that petrifying pep-talk.

I walked up to the teller's window; cheesing from ear to ear I asked, for Karen Johnson. The branch manager had been waiting for me. She walked out from her glass-enclosed office space in faded black dress pants and a too little peach blouse.

Once we made it to her office, before either of us sat down, she shook my hand and reintroduced herself. That's when I graciously told her my name was Victoria Lewis.

Karen was young, unkempt and her hair was greasy. When I looked down at her feet, all I could think was, *Father, she should never wear her unpolished, crusty feet out.*

Karen's office smelled like hot corn chips and four hours of musty sweaty workout panties. Then she shut the door to make matters worse.

Hurry up with my cash so I can leave, I thought, gasping for air in this unprofessional and unsanitary office.

She asked for my license and another form of ID.

"Are you opening an account, Ms. Lewis?"

Hell, naw but you can open this damn door.

"No thank you," I said displaying sassiness.

That pep-talk got me feeling bullish!

Karen took my check and wrote my information on it, then she handed it back, which startled me, but it was only to sign the back. I flamboyantly signed the back of my check.

Karen requested another banker to come and sign off on the large transaction. I had no idea a person could strut into a bank and cash this sort of check. Mr. Lane knew how to do everything. After that, she escorted me to a teller who counted my money at least five times. They counted it on the money counter like three times as I rubbernecked and tailed it with them. Before I left, they strived even harder to convince me to open an account with that bank, even telling me it wasn't safe to have that much cash on me.

As I strutted my stuff out of the bank, it crossed my mind that no one questioned me why Mr. Lane had written me such a large check. *Nobody.*

I walked out of Mr. Lane's bank with fifty thousand dollars in a secondhand five-dollar purse. That money was too heavy so, I bumped *"Gucci Mane, Heavy."* With my Impala on two wheels, I skyrocketed across town to my bank Walls Cargo to deposit the money and, like clockwork, Mr. Lane called.

He commanded me not to deposit all that money into my account at once. Karen and the other bank employees had been fretful about me having so much cash on me. Truth be told, Mr. Lane boss'd me up with my private security. Mr. Lane protected himself and me in a way.

I questioned Mr. Lane in a friendly voice, about what I needed to do, as if I no longer feared him. He then instructed me to deposit only ten thousand or less and place the rest in a safe deposit box.

"Where do I get a safe deposit box from?"

"Do you know anything about money?" He was agitated. I could hear the frustration in his voice.

"No, I don't," I said still feeling bullish.

Shockingly, he humbled himself again and told me to purchase the safe deposit box from my bank.

I whipped into the bank with one hand as if I was driving a brand-new Cadillac. In high-spirits, I bounced out of my car, digging the scene looking for Mr. Lane since he could see me, but I didn't see him, and I had no clue whom he could have following me. I walked into the Walls Cargo bank and waited in line with a purse full of money. Slowly, I was becoming happy and excited about my new life.

Finally, it was my turn to see the teller. The excitement and nervousness made me forget to count out ten thousand to deposit in my account. She didn't smell like the other banker, and she was well groomed from what I could see from where she was sitting.

The teller, in a navy-blue-and-white striped blouse, greeted me as soon as I walked up to the counter. I asked her for a deposit slip once I tried to estimate how much I had on the bank counter.

"You know when you deposit money over ten thousand dollars, it is questioned by the feds," she said. *I almost pissed my britches!* Mr. Lane just instructed me to count the money beforehand. Instead, I guesstimated because I forgot to, count. I softly whispered and told her to give me my money back, all but nine thousand dollars.

I told her to suspend that transaction immediately.

I leaned in closer to whisper to her. "If you do so without a scene and getting loudmouthed, Ole, Benjamin Franklin right is yours."

We completed the transaction, and I slid her that, Ole, Benjamin Franklin. Mr. Lane coached me, to get a safe deposit box. This time I didn't forget, nor did I guesstimate. I placed all the money in a safe deposit box except for five thousand dollars. I brought that money home and hid it in books.

When I used to sell marijuana, I purchased two diversion book safes from an online store. The book safes resembled a real book, just like the ones I had seen in all the Gangster Movies I often watched. However, these had more space cut in the center. Most pilfers don't read, and a book would be the last place any of them would look. *I reckon, Mr. Lane taught me a word, pilfer.*

I stayed up most of the night tucking away my Benji's into the books. Occasionally, I peeked through the blinds looking outside for Mr. Lane or his acquaintances. Every time I looked through the blinds and stared into the compacted apartment parking lot, I thought to myself, *Mr. Lane is the real plug.*

CHAPTER

NINE

*O*n Saturday morning, Mona and I went house shopping. I finally found an old subdivision I adored after I went looking for a home in Madison. This is predominantly where most rich white people reside.

This is where I shopped for my groceries. Troubling times in my past pushed me out here to grocery shop, because only in Jackson, when someone had a buggy full of brand-name groceries, they had to be on food stamps. In Madison, it was different. No one knew me, and no one thought I was on food stamps.

My dream was to purchase a home in the largest white populated neighborhood in Mississippi, and it was Madison, just because they used to make it so difficult for us blacks to purchase a home in their populated areas. I bet my bottom dollar if these white people knew another white person had given me the capital to transition into their neighborhood, a new riot and war would have broken out.

I understood nothing about purchasing a home, and I couldn't ask my mom or anyone in my family to assist, because they couldn't know what business I was involved in.

Back in the day I had driven through many neighborhoods every time I went to the supermarket. After driving around for a while, I found my dream home – in a gated community. Fortunately, as I veered in, another car had already put the code in. Therefore, I followed them into the neighborhood. Mona arose in her car seat as we drove around looking. She had taste.

A modern, antique-looking, two-story brick house trimmed in white caught my eye. Super tall, whitish brick columns and a three-car garage made me slam on the breaks. I pulled into the driveway, immediately taking Mona out her car seat. I attached her on my hip as I walked around the house looking through fogged windows.

She was jumping up and down glancing into any visible rooms. Mona thought it was a game. Her giggle was too cute! Time stalled as I watched the happiness of Mona running around the yard. *Home sweet home!* I thought to myself.

No future anxieties of speeding vehicles or careless drivers hitting Mona, just in case she chased a ball, balloon or even a butterfly into the apartment complex parking lot. My baby girl's legs could remain cheerleader-flawless from concrete scrapes and bruises if she's clumsy. In my train of thought, she would be given equal opportunities to cheer, model or show off scar-less legs while running track.

If the house fell through, Mona could then be in pursuit of breezes to cool her off in this Mississippi heat while zooming around on her big wheels on low-cut grass. One day, I shall soon prepare lunch under the abandoned spider web infested covered patio. Yuck!

The patio contained all the bells and whistles including a corroded outdoor stainless steel kitchen. Still, I pictured myself sitting at the brick island, sipping sweet lemonade. My favorite!

On chilly days, the fireplace would keep us warm as we snuggle up while I read one of Mona's favorite books. I also see this murky, nasty green pool had been neglected, but a gated remodeled pool will motivate Mona and I both to take swimming lessons.

She will not be another, *"Black people can't swim static and drown."*

Owning a home contributed to Mona's future. The decisions I make now dictate her life just as much as mine. *"Mother,"* most important role of many. I am the security guard in charge of securing her well-being.

Mona's role model, first hero, provider, nurse, chuffer, boyfriend fighter, listening ear, crying partner, chef, number one fan, teacher maid and personal ATM. Time will place many more labels on me.

Providing a better life now prepared *"Mother"* for upcoming roles.

I tossed Mona over my shoulder, pretending to fly with her. A soaring young mom from side to side enjoying some of the good life with the one I gave life had been a priceless and wonderful feeling. I walked to the front and took my phone out of my back pocket. I gathered the information from the for-sale sign, hoping to contact someone to purchase this property soon.

I dialed the number on the sign and Jack Simpson, the realtor, answered.

"Jack Simpson."

"Hi Mr. Simpson, how are you today?"

"I'm well. Thanks for asking."

"Uh, yes, my name is Victoria. I'm calling to inquire about the property for sale on 77577 Johnstone Drive."

He revealed that a mortgage approval letter was necessary.

"How do I get that?" I asked. Before he could answer my question, he promptly told me he would call me back.

I no longer had worries about bills, but it seemed I might have newer worries.

I called Jack for a week, and he didn't return my calls.

I drove back to 77577 Johnstone Drive and this time I retrieved all the information off the sign. I looked up the real estate company Cold-all Max-Dan and made it my business to get up early Monday morning to visit him.

Almost a month after Mr. Lane had given me the money, I acted and travelled to Jack's office first thing in the morning. When I pulled up to the office building, I walked up to the front door that had an intercom system connected to it. I pressed the bell button and the receptionist answered.

"I'm here to see Mr. Jack Simpson," I said.

"Come on in. Take the elevator up to the first floor."

When I arrived at the first floor, Mr. Simpson was standing at the receptionist desk waiting for me. The size of his stomach articulated exactly how slothful and full he was. He was hungry for money and food, and I was hungry for that Johnstone House. He ought to preserve that same passion and help me purchase that property.

The Dockers pants and matching shirt with the cleaner's tag hanging out at the collar hinted he had to be a professional. His face didn't say he was delighted to see me; however, his action reflected *"let me make it snappy because this youngster is a waste of my time."*

I followed the middle-aged frat boy while eyeing his balding head. Thinking to myself *shave it off and go bald. Alternatively, buy a wig like Mrs. Benton.* He still had an appealing tight butt and his brown loafers were spotless. He was a well-groomed man with a beer gut.

As soon as we marched into his office, I told him I was Victoria Lewis, and I had been phoning him. This time I did all the conversing. Jack reminded me, as if I had forgotten, that I needed a pre-approval letter before I could view the property.

"How do I get a mortgage approval letter?"

He laughed arrogantly. "You need to be pre-approved by either a bank or mortgage origination company to obtain the letter. Are you currently working with a mortgage company to purchase a home, Ms. Lewis?"

"No, and I have no knowledge of what to do or whom to speak to, and you may refer to me as Victoria going forward."

"Victoria, do understand you have to actually possess funds or some form of funding to purchase a home?"

I stared him dead in his eyes and used one of Mr. Lane's favorite lines. "Money isn't an issue."

"Victoria, the more expensive the home, the more down-payment you will have to have."

I bluntly told Jack, "Whether you sell me that property or not, if I desire it, I will certainly purchase it. Now, Jack, you can either profit or take a loss, but I am purchasing 7577 Johnstone." He peculiarly glanced at me, then he rotated his office chair around to his computer.

The house I wanted was three hundred and ten thousand dollars. It had been appraised for over four hundred thousand. The current owner purchased it below market value as a foreclosed property. Since it required numerous cosmetic repairs to the inside, outside and the pool, it had been underpriced for a quick sale.

"Victoria, to purchase the Johnstone property, it's essential that you've earned an income, well over a hundred thousand dollars per year for the last two years." I hadn't been employed long enough to provide the requested income documentation. "Now let's be straightforward, Victoria, how do you have ready money but no documentation supporting your earnings?"

I didn't react. I played it cool while he continued to yap his mouth.

"Victoria, you're young and some things you will not understand."

Jack sounded like the Benton's and Mr. Lane with the direction I assumed this conversation was headed.

Jack continued by saying, "Money can buy just about anything Victoria. If I can entrust in you to never disclose how or who assisted you in obtaining this loan, documents to provide to the underwriters and a cashier's check for your down-payment, closing cost and pre-paid fees, etc. then guess what Victoria, Johnstone will be yours to purchase, now can I trust you?"

"Yes, sir, you can." My palms became clammy again. Jack spoke the same language of the Benton's and Mr. Lane. It always started with "Can I trust you?" and ended with money. However, I knew Mr. Simpson was on to me, and he knew that my cash wasn't legit. Furthermore, I now knew he wasn't a law-abiding, by the book's citizen either.

What am I getting myself into? I thought.

"I know a few big shots that could furnish some tax returns, create a business for you and whatever else the underwriters request," he said. "Let me make a quick phone call." He stepped out of the room.

He marched back into the office a short while later. "Now, Victoria, I need your absolute word that I can sleep at night knowing you will never disclose to anyone how you obtained the loan."

"Yes, you have my word, I will never disclose to anyone how I purchased my home," I said.

"Okay Victoria you're preparing to enter a world of privilege that many young black women are never inducted into; consider yourself preordained," Jack conceitedly told me.

I asked Jack in a fishy way, "This new world I am entering; does it embrace fly-fishing and stringing-up largemouth black bass?"

"Victoria, you're just full of beans; your energetic spirit and now rib-tickling humor is unbeatable," Jack cackled. He had no awareness of what in the heck I was referring to about fly-fishing, stringing-up or largemouth black bass. This had given me a sense of relief because I couldn't stomach another Mr. Lane

Therefore, I told Jack, "Thank you for the unique compliment and most importantly a peaceful non-threatening understanding."

Jack chuckled saying, "Thank you Victoria. Come. Follow me." He motioned me to follow him outside to the parking lot. We both got in our vehicles and hopped on Interstate 55 heading south. I trailed his black Mercedes close, pursuing him so close that sometimes I was bumper to bumper with him! Brake light to brake light.

We drove into a popular car dealership off I-55 that's well known to be one of the larger ones in the Jackson Metropolitan area. He escorted me into the office of a another hungry, beer gut white man. Oh yeah! They had to be fraternity brothers. Matching Budweiser beer guts were a tell-tale sign.

Before the man said hello or anything, he said to Jack, *"Close the door, you're letting all the good air out."* He was certified country. They slammed the door behind me as if I was about to be inaugurated into the country folk mafia. We only missed the 'Big Boss,' Mr. Lane.

Jack familiarized me to the "MAN" named Bradley. He reminded me of the clean-cut stout guys my cousin Sabrina use to court. Those pot-bellied male pigs were often chased out the house by Zaka. Hefty and round in the waist, but smooth-tongued, charismatic and bearded, merging to create a sexy ass "Big Daddy." His cologne smelled powerful. It ignited the room. Strong.

He was stuck with this property and wanted to dump it soon, but he did not bank on dumping to a young girl like MOI. In my eyes, this was the picture-perfect situation for MOI.

Desperate situations make people such as Bradley do desperate things such as induct me, a young girl, into a world I never knew even existed.

Mr. Lane had promised me more money once Mrs. Lane expired, so I wanted to take a chance on buying this house.

Bradley leaned back in his brown and gold oversized leather office chair after he scrutinized me and said,

"Well butter my butt and call me a biscuit Jack, she's still wet behind the ears."

Jack threw his hand up and bowed his head to the side as he agreed with Bradley without saying a word.

Jack then said, "Bradley, Victoria's her name, and she's perfect for this property; I trust her enough to let her in on our business and close this deal."

Bradley laughed and sarcastically said,

"There's more than one way to skin a cat and Jack you can slap yo mama because you always find it."

Bradley was a country talking fool, but he tickled me, I liked him. We were introduced without being introduced, as we unexplainably called one another by first our first names. Bradley elevated his beer gut up in his chair and said,

"Victoria, are you ready to run with the big dogs, or you wanna stay under the porch?"

I told Bradly in a gutsy respectable way,

"Bradley, I been jumped off the porch and I was born to run with the big dogs."

Bradley then replied, trying to ensure I was ready,

"Now Victoria, don't you piss on my leg and tell me it's raining.

Because that dog won't hunt."

"Sir, I have dreamed of days like this to sit in an office preparing to purchase my dream home for my daughter and myself; just please trust me enough to grant me this opportunity to purchase your property," I emotional said to Bradley.

Bradley then said,

"Darling, I reckon I can relate, as my own family was so poor, they couldn't jump over a nickel to save a dime.

Therefore Victoria, if the creek doesn't rise, you will have your dream home."

"Thank you so much, Bradley and Jack," I said, shaking their hands and bowing my head back and forth as a gesture of being gracious. That went better than I could have ever imagined. *Bradley never threw prejudice or racist remarks at me. He talked without mentioning the color of my skin, for once a human-to-human conversation where color was not part of the topic of conversation.*

Shortly after I said thank you, a lady named Lacy was called to Bradley's office. She was young, but older looking than me. Lacy was eye-catching, because she gripped your attention when you eyeballed her struggling to bend and sit in her too tight pants.

Bradley instructed her to gather all my information, at times getting agitated with her, especially, when he had to repeat repeated the same thing constantly. I could have had her job. Jack finally spoke up, as he had become mute while Bradley and I conversed.

Jack asked me how did I make a living? I told him I was a private caregiver. They looked at each other as if an ass wiper couldn't swipe a three-hundred-thousand-dollar, home. Jack then instructed Lacy to create a sitting service as a business for me.

Since Mr. Lane always called me his black Ma'Sitter, I named my new business Ma'Sitter Care Services. Lacy said very little; she just jotted down whatever she was told.

They ordered Lacy to have my new business registered with the state, so it was incorporated. It would be a legit business. I would be legal. That was easy. I could also employ other sitters and take more clients if I desired to.

Jack and Bradley both agreed the hard part was coming up with the back, tax payment. They told me I had to amend my taxes for the prior two years plus be able to pay all the back taxes. Jack said I could set up a payment arrangement with the IRS, but I had to have the returns stamped, dated and signed by the IRS tax agent to prove the taxes were amended.

That was a lengthy meeting. Jack and Bradley then sent Lacy to get started.

Once she left the office, Bradley said,

"Her britches were so tight you could see her religion."

Jack, that damn Lacy of ours is about as useful as a steering wheel on a mule."

While they were laughing about Lacy, I had been thinking about my cash flow. Mr. Lane had promised me more cash once Mrs. Lane expired, so I wanted to take a chance on purchasing this house. However, now I needed cash for a down-payment and back taxes payment.

That night, I stayed up thinking about how I could get more money to pay the IRS and the down payment. Then it hit me. I could play the Benton's and Mr. Lane.

CHAPTER

TEN

*M*r. Lane was poisoning his arsenic. The toxin was colorless and odorless. He was only administrating her tiny doses of what I viewed to be arsenic so that she would not croak momentarily. He desired it to appear as if her poor health was naturally declining. Her petite, frail body would not tolerate a great deal. The good people always wind up in bad hands.

Mrs. Lane had never been problematic. She managed to make my days laid-back. Sometimes while cleansing her, I knew those fragile bones hurt, rolling from side to side as I softly sponged her blistering bedsores. Mr. Lane declined to change her soiled diaper more often.

I came up with a plan to empty the bottle full of arsenic poison and to fill it with water and olive oil. Since the bottle was a dark glass object, he would never see the oil floating in the water, but the oil gave the water a smell.

The next morning, I told Mr. Lane it was taking too long and that I was offered a better-paying job. Instantaneously, his face transformed bloodshot, his mouth trembled as he raised his voice calling me deceitful. Mr. Lane placed fear in my heart that made me shut the hell up.

"Do you think I don't know what you have been up to?" Even though he calmed back down. Mr. Lane still startled me when he told me where the property was that I wanted to purchase. He knew I required more funding and he knew all the looping around I had been doing. "Gal, you have been busy and persistent. I don't have many colored friends, hell I don't have none to think about it, but if I had to pick one, I would pick you over and over," he told me. Thinking, *"Is this a compliment or an insult?"* Either way, I will take it right with another check, thinking to myself.

"Initially, I didn't like you because you're colored," Mr. Lane went on to say. "Then I gathered, this young gal is intelligent, but blind. You don't see none of the brick walls that were built to keep you out intentionally."

I might have had the hunger for the same materialistic belongings as Mr Lane, but I wasn't an old lady hitter sitter.

He asked how much more I needed, and I was afraid to say the amount. I just knew he would tell me I had lost my motherfucking mind.

However, I held my breath, and I told him that the fifty thousand dollars would be spent because I had to settle -up with the IRS to get the house.

"Money is not a problem Victoria," he said, just as I predicted.

That morning, he wrote me out a check for $150,000. This was unbelievable and I would have never expected Mr. Lane out of the billions of people on this earth to be the one person that made my dream of Homeownership come to reality.

"You're my Ma'Sitter," Victoria. I can't pull this off without ya'." No one would ever believe a white man was giving me $350,000.00 when it's all said and done, just to put his wife to sleep.

No one would ever understand the authenticated significance of Ma'Sitter.

Mr. Lane told me again. "Once she is in the ground," he said, "I will give you another $150,000.00 from the insurance; and your baby, Mona, should never be on welfare either."

I had enough bread now to make a settlement with the IRS.

CHAPTER

ELEVEN

*T*he next day, I hurried to the IRS office on Capitol to file the taxes prepared for MOI. There was much red tape I had to go through to purchase that property and paying the IRS in full wasn't the only step. Jack and Bradley from the car dealership introduced me to Shaun. Shaun was my mortgage originator.

Damn. I thought I was done after the IRS office.

I travelled across town to link-up with Shaun after I left the IRS office, and I didn't get the news I envisioned. Buying a house was challenging, and it was taxing my stash of cash. He advised me it's a necessity to run my credit and that he required my social security number.

Damn. My mom has all that information.

After calling my mom and answering fifty thousand of her questions about why I demanded my information, I provided Shaun what he required. He pulled my credit report. I quickly identified this to become a hindrance. I didn't possess any credit. All I had reporting on my credit report was a Chevy Impala.

Shaun received a hit back. "Miss Lewis, you're maintaining a textbook score," he happily stated. "This is one of the most uncomplicated loans I've prepared in a while." I lifted-up in his chair thunderstruck.

"How?"

"Ms. Lewis, your credit score is 781. Come around and look yourself." And, sure enough, it was all my information.

"Click on the auto loans," I demanded him. The Chevy Impala was my loan, but the other car loan belonged to the vehicle I drove in high school. My mom hassled me, ensuring I paid for that vehicle even when she confiscated it from me when I considered myself grown and aspired to be out on my own.

Wow. I caught what he threw out now.

Once I knew for certain that would be my residence, I asked Jack if he could meet me one day at the address of the house to show my family. Jack assured me I no longer had to contact him to view my, soon-to-be new residence. So, he furnished me the code to the lockbox and said I could come as I pleased, even though we had not closed yet.

Sunday was the perfect day to beg my family to meet me in Johnston after church. So, once the entire gang arrived, I raced my sister, Zoey, like a kid to the French mahogany double doors to unlock the lockbox. While I was obtaining the key, I gazed back over my shoulder to observe Zoey checking out my gas French Market lanterns. Once I unlocked my door, they all kind of hesitated to follow me.

So, they questioned whose house this was and why they were here. I enthusiastically expressed to them that this was my new residence. They all arrogantly cackled and ranted and raved all sorts of crap.

Like, *"Girl you need to stop lying."*

"This is a house you're going to clean."

"I hope you didn't let these people shortchange you."

"Do not be desperate and accept any amount of money to clean this big house."

Nobody would step a foot inside. I tried my best to convince these people, my so-called family that I was becoming a first- time homeowner. After a while, I said fuc'em and locked the property up without even re-entering. This was the main reason I didn't intend on disclosing my personal business with anyone. Plus, I wanted nobody but God judging me.

After my family dismantled my feelings, I primarily hung by the phone to hear something about closing on my house. Two weeks went by, and every day that money burned my pocket more and more. Trying not to squander my dough was so tough though. However, I splurged on cable and all-of-a sudden, every cotton-picking commercial advertised sale. So, I had the cable for the first time voluntarily discounted.

After an elongated wait, I heard the news I had been anticipating – that I had been finally scheduled to close on Johnstone by the end of the week. *Oh my God, this is real. I am on the books to be a young black homeowner and illustrate to my family I was ordained to live lavish.*

I am a new money-making rich bitch! Just like Mrs. Benton

The next morning, Jack had instructed me to meet him at the bank. I had to hand-over a chunk of my cash for the down payment in exchange for a cashier's check. This was part of closing. I went window shopping for new furnishings. My closing was just two days away, but I still couldn't fritter away any dead presidents just if something unpredictable occurred.

At last, I closed. It was so time-consuming having to sign all those papers. However, well worth it, because The American Dream of Homeownership was accomplished. Still in disbelief, but wished my champ, Zaka, could witness this ridiculous home. Prosperity and wealth had been in my DNA. Zaka repeatedly told me I would be superior! I salute him and all the certainty he lectured as he foresaw it.

Victoria, "The Hitter Sitter," must have been in my DNA.

When I could splurge and get the ball rolling on remodeling my new extravagant pad- that's what I concentrated on. Renovating a house was beyonddddd me — way more labor than I had anticipated. Explaining to my family with the rehearsed white lie that Jack and Bradley concocted had been even trickier. Jack, Bradley and Mr. Lane all realized people would question how I acquired this home. Fib to my friends and family while fixing up my house. Fib and fix that's all I knew to do.

Jack and Bradley coached me on how to persuade people if they ever inquired about how I purchased such an expensive property. The tale to be spoken was that I had been compensated a large amount of cash to purchase this property. Mr. Lane approved of this trumped-up-story and added to it. He had been involved with the entire process.

He scrutinized my paperwork before my closing, ensuring I wasn't taken advantage of, like them sticking me with a floating interest rate, fake appraisal or misappropriating too much of my funds for the down payment. Mr. Lane counseled me regarding all the mortgage fraud. That had been under the radar but was successfully making money. I acknowledged the fact he refused to watch someone hustle me out of the cheddar he disbursed me.

Mr. Lane tolerated me being off from duty at their residence as much as I desired. I barely monitored the progression the arsenic poison was taking on Mrs. Lane. I had no knowledge of her missed or kept dialysis appointments, if bedsores covered her butt or of him

118 | LATOYA LAWSON

not changing her adulterated diapers. For all I knew, she could be deceased and halfway decomposed.

I had only filled that one bogus bottle of arsenic poison. Those fresh green Benji's had me wrapped-up in renovating my mini mansion like "MTV Cribs." Decking it out! My interior decorator, Rachel, persuaded me to purchase furniture I couldn't pronounce nor spell. *Expensive foreign shit! Stamps on your passport shit.* I even considered purchasing a foreign new vehicle. Mrs. Lane drifted further and further away from my mind, as well as this world.

Wealth is so addictive, especially when you go from barely having enough to having more than enough. People handle you differently when you have bread.

Mr. Lane changed my life, but his wife's life was the crucial sacrifice. My days of becoming a new hitter sitter were slowly numbered. No matter how I tried not to think of it that way, it was that way. I would be a murderer, just like Mr. Lane. He wanted her unresponsive within two weeks, and it was now three weeks after my last payment.

Every time my phone and doorbell rang, I just knew it was Mr. Lane or the police. I was so paranoid; it took much adjusting and leveling up to this lifestyle. The Benton's remained oblivious about my brand-new life and wealth. I had been feeding them bullshit for months. I would tell them,

"Mr. Lane still isn't changing her at night; however, she has no new bedsores."

"She has dropped more weight; then again the damage from her stroke does not allow her a normal appetite."

"Yes, Mr. Lane is verbally abusive towards her, but on the other hand, she does fuss back by mumbling."

"No, he is not physically abusive, if so, it's no physical evidence in plain sight."

"He does not feed her, but in spite of this, I do."

"I even make her fattening Boost Shakes daily."

Regardless, whatever I relayed to them, the crusade to save Mrs. Lane was almost terminated. On the other hand, since I didn't need the Benton's "Lil weekly hundred dollars," I gifted it to Sallie every week. I trailed her home one Thursday and once she drove into her driveway in the ghetto, knew I had made an honorable decision. Sallie and I conversed about the Benton's and how important it was for her to never mention to them I had been gifting her money weekly alternatively, that we even knew each other.

Sallie was overjoyed, and it thrilled me to bits and pieces benefitting someone else besides myself. Weekly, I did my pick up on Fridays from the Benton's and delivered it to Sallie with a gift card of some sort.

Like a nail shop, beauty shop, make-up, supermarket, clothing store, gas station, movies, restaurant gift card, etc., Sallie appeared every Friday as a different woman. She was transitioning into a beautiful, well-kept black woman.

Finally, her black had stopped cracking, and she was smiling again, especially, when I purchased her some teeth. I did all sorts of generous deeds for my family and close friends.

Not over-the-top or wasteful good-deeds, but things people needed. Like a light bill paid, new furniture, rent paid a few months, birthday gifts and I never took the credit. I remained anonymous, because if people knew I had money like that to trick off, I would be broke, within months.

My acts of kindness took creativity and deep thoughts. While I was out playing Santa, Mrs. Lane was transitioning to the pearly white gates of Heaven.

CHAPTER

TWELVE

*M*rs. Lane perished on a Thursday night. Mr. Lane summoned me over when she grasped her last breath. When I arrived at the Lane's, I was shaking. I had only seen a dead body at funerals and on TV. As I approached the door, my hands started sweating. I rang the doorbell, and my wet finger slid back off. It caused the doorbell to ring quickly.

Mr. Lane greeted me with a big ass smile.

I slowly followed Mr. Lane as we headed towards Mrs. Lane's bedroom and I was scared out of my wits.

Her lifeless body laid on the cold floor and her adult diaper was halfway off. She barely had on her nightgown. Mr. Lane demanded I assist him in cleaning her up.

"Pick her up, place her back in the bed. Get her dressed."

"I ain't doing that shit!" Grandma Louise always told us to let the dead souls rest. Mrs. Lane's light-blue, naked body rested on the floor, full of toxins. Vomit and all things dead covered her pineapple-printed nightgown, bile covered her high cheekbones.

Her hair strands were camouflaged with bile, vomit and milky saliva foam. You could distinguish she choked on her milky saliva, then vomit and I guess bile last. The combination of odors caused me to heave, trying not to puke. I held my breath. The beige carpet had dark brownish pee stains instead of yellow. That soaked in as her body lay on top.

Her wide opened dead eyes stared right at me as I bent over to examine her. Mrs. Lane was in complete agony, especially if she witnessed her husband celebrating as she breathed her last breath. Alternatively, maybe she abruptly kicked the bucket while the angels snapped their fingers yelling, "chop-chop," for the most beautiful heaven on earth soul.

As I was detecting the real-life crime scene, Mr. Lane dared to advise me this was what I got paid for. *No, the hell it wasn't either.* He solicited me to vouch for him, not to touch a cold, light baby blue, perished Mrs. Lane.

We went back and forth for a minute, quarreling about my job description. Mr. Lane had under no circumstances mentioned me partaking in touching or re-touching her perished spirit as part of our verbal agreement. Quarreling with him at this point had been impractical. I got what I wanted and needed. He was no longer my boss; I had money now just like him. Both of us grew even more nauseous, but still quarreling one word at a time. Saying, "No," and "Yes." Clasping our noses and spraying. So, the back, fourth wasn't squished until I surrendered.

After we scrubbed and decontaminated her, I realized handling a dead body was not as dreadful as I anticipated. Mr. Lane validated why she had been on the floor. The final dose of arsenic was abundant, and she initially had an uncontrollable seizure. Mrs. Lane jiggled, quivered and bobbed her head on the wooden headboard, so severely that he had to toss her already deadweight stroke body on the beige carpet flooring to prevent her from splitting parts of the wooden bed, ripping the comforter or destroying any other antique furniture.

However, we had to suspend our conversation and speed this process up, as her body had undergone a rapid change in color. By the time we completed purification, she was nippy. We boosted-up her heavy, dead weight back onto the bed. Before we placed her back in, we replaced the contaminated sheets, making it pleasant, soft, cottony and fluffy; I also bedecked the side she didn't utilize.

I originated the plan to position two blanket warmers on her. We attired Mrs. Lane in her beloved four shades of the pink robe and matching gown, coordinated with some fuzzy pink and thick white socks. We had fashioned her to appear elaborate. Therefore, she would give the impression to anyone's naked eye to have been in good physical health. I then masked her blue, cold to touch, pale face with concealer. I even shut her eyes to apply the brown eyeliner and mascara. Those high cheekbones previously smeared with vomit, now flaunted daubed on red blush, just the way she loved it.

I even splashed her with a little perfume. Once we clothed her and relaxed her stiff body gracefully in the bed, we then labored on the filthy floor. The stench of vomit, bile and urine caused me to barf. Fortunately, I reached the toilet and not the floor first.

At last, we were done sanitizing, decontaminating and scrubbing the room; we phoned the doctor's office, but no one answered. Once Dr. Gilbert called back, we notified him that Mrs. Lane had passed away in her sleep. Mr. Lane sobbed as if he was moaning his wife while informing the doctor; he assumed she experienced a seizure.

The good doc ordered Mr. Lane to arrange for the undertakers to come. Once the undertakers retrieved the corpse, Dr. Gilbert assured Mr. Lane he would release the death certificate. If the doctor issued the death certificate, then no investigation would be implemented.

I hate to utter this, but I intended for her death to be prevented, but I also preferred the payout. This had been the biggest dilemma. Either I had to take a life and get rich or save one and remain poor. The Benton's had aimed to rescue her, but it was too late. They wanted control over her estate just as much as Mr. Lane.

One night, I sat up and figured out the difference between the Mr. Lane and the Benton's. Mr. Lane gained much more by murdering his wife – much more money and a large insurance payout.

The Benton's only sought after her so Mr. Lane couldn't recoup the insurance policy if she is unexpectedly deceased. Plus, they would regain control over Mrs. Lane's personal life. I still had to play the young, gullible, blackberry- girl role with the Benton's.

Therefore, I phoned the Benton's after I left the Lane's residence. Having to convey to them she had perished- shattered my heart into pieces. Mrs. Benton had prearranged for the State Department of Health to come and remove her. In just a few more days, I would never know the evidence they had acquired. All I knew of was that I was not the Benton's real B.U.S.

I was astonished; the Benton's only inquired about what way had she departed this life.

"A seizure in her sleep."

"I'll give her sister a ring," Mrs. Benton's sorrowfully said.

I comforted myself by convincing myself she was in terrible condition, on top of being in deadly hands from the day she said I do for the second time, however, to the wrong man, twice.

The next day, I called Mr. Lane and asked about the funeral. Mrs. Lane was already on the books to be cremated sometime that day. He didn't deem it necessary to hold a church service or a graveside service. Mrs. Lane's only sister wouldn't be flown-out until the following Monday anyhow. Mr. Lane considered the fact that she had no children and no real close family here in Mississippi. Therefore, there wasn't a reason to waste money on a funeral.

Mrs. Lane had no write-up in the newspaper like her prior husband. Quite Frankly, she basically met her maker lonely and in the hands of a piggish murderer. The Benton's invited me over, but I declined. By creating an excuse that Mona was ill with a stomach bug. I still drove by the Benton's home, and I asked Mr. Lane to monitor them, since he was acquainted with my two-faced, B.U.S (Black Underpaid Snitch) double-dealing life.

The Benton's attempted to stir-up some noise by spreading and fabricating the rumormonger that Mr. Lane murdered Mrs. Lane. Without proof, it was just a gossipmonger that attempted to become worthy of a newsmonger. They tried to entangle me in the tittle-tattle, and that's when it came crashing down.

Black sitters' do not murder patients just for the hell of it. We keep them alive! Hell, we necessitate our paychecks and jobs. A dead patient's corpse does not pay bills, so I thought. Black sitters are not intelligent enough to make a substantial living from becoming a "Hitter Sitter," so, they thought.

The Benton's strived for another avenue by saying, "Mr. Lane paid her only sister off to keep her mouth harnessed." I had never encountered Mrs. Lane sister. Another cock-and-bill story that did not stick. Mr. Lane had gotten away with murder. Even though the

Benton's raised suspicion, eyebrows and much conversation around town, it wasn't enough evidence to warrant probable cause. Furthermore, it did not halt the Benton's social life, money and swinging. I pulled a Mr. Lane by tailing them in unmarked cars occasionally.

Two months had gone by since Mrs. Lane's death, and my first couple of months with no work kept me thinking. *How in the world did I end up with this big ass house?* I shook off the thought. I struggled to move on with my life and to disregard that well-hidden secret I devoured. "Triple C," did nothing for my conscience. Church, prayers and reading my Bible contributed to temporary relief. Splurging, vacations, weave and expensive spoiling of Mona produced new habits. Spending habits! High-priced temporary relief!

For the next two years, I grieved Mrs. Lane. I didn't labor as a caregiver or sitter anymore. Instead, I employed people to work for me through my business. I couldn't stomach it any longer. My none-peaceful life held me accountable for what I had done to Mrs. Lane.

CHAPTER

THIRTEEN

It had been three years since Mrs. Lane's death. I was still living off Mr. Lane's money, but it was getting low. I wondered how many people exterminated loved ones for monetary gain. Contemplating, maybe I was not the only hitter Ma'Sitter indulging in this lifestyle.

Hopefully, my children wouldn't kill me for my money.

I was fortunate as hell that my business succeeded, and I was still sitting on a little cash.

One day, I entertained a call from Mr. Lane. He said he would love to unite. Three years had vanished by, and he wanted to chitchat. I didn't desire to visit with him at all, but I arranged it anyway. What if something came up? What if it was developing information about his wife's death I needed to know about?

I drove up to the same house his wife took her last breath in, and to my amazement, he had company, another white man and woman.

What the hell is going on? Mr. Lane introduced me as his Ma'Sitter. The couple introduced themselves as Mr. and Mrs. Mizkeli.

"Victoria, these are my good friends, Mr. and Mrs. Mizkeli," said Mr. Lane. "They're looking for someone to sit with their mother."

Oh shit, I thought. *I know what this is, but I don't know if I can do it again. I am barely getting over Mrs. Lane's death.*

"Victoria. Nice to meet you both." I smiled reluctantly. My palms were sweating. "I don't sit with people anymore. I hire sitters to work for me. I can get someone good for you," I insisted.

"We request you, Victoria. We need you to aid us like you aided Mr. Lane. We heard your services are top notch," Mr. Mizkelli winked at me. I pretended as if I had no understanding of what he was chattering about.

"We need you." He took another sip of brandy from his glass cup and sat it down on the counter. "We're willing to pay double for your services."

I stopped him dead in his tracks.

"I am done sitting. I only hire sitters and if you would like, I can personally recommend one of my sitters for your mom, Mr.

Mizkeli." I was finished with this shit. I couldn't do it anymore. My head was all fucked up from the last case I had.

"Victoria, can I speak to you outside, please?"

Mr. Mizkeli and I walked towards the front porch and stood near Mr. Lane's old, white, wooden rocking chair. Mr. Mizkeli said to me, "I need you to live with my mother and take care of her the way you took care of Mrs. Lane."

He assured me she was very wealthy. He wanted someone capable of doing this quickly and quietly. A professional. I cleared my throat when he referred to me as a professional.

"If you say yes now, tomorrow you'll have 250,000.00 dollars in cash. No one will ever know. Now, I've heard nothing but positive things about your Ma'Sitter service; and for a black woman your age, this is much money." This man identified all my business and my weaknesses.

"Trust me. You'll never experience another opportunity to make this much tax-free money." That grasped my attention. Now he knew what he was gibbering about. There were not many 'Mr. Lane's' running around Mississippi. Mr. Mizkeli was another - lifetime opportunity.

I hesitated in saying no, which meant it was a yes. Mr. Lane done turned me into a contract killer giving out references and shit. *He ain't getting a cut. Nor a referral fee. This could be a setup; who's to say Mr. Lane ain't turned fed? The only way to trap a bird in a cage is to feed them more bread. Here I am being hoggish!*

Mr. Lane would assassinate himself before he turned fed. He wasn't built like that. I had been around him long enough to know. "Imma do it," I told him!

Tomorrow he would have 250,000.00 dollars in cash for me, and once she was deceased, he would have another 250,000 for me; and no one would ever know.

He blabbed so long about why I should exterminate his mother that I was convinced. *This bitch needed to be exterminated!* I agreed to do the job. This was a live-in sitter gig.

These people were going to glory anyway because they were ailing and aging. That's what I kept uttering to myself. *I'm not performing any ill-treatment if they are already ill. I'm just assisting.*

The next day, Mr. Mizkeli dropped off 250,000.00 in cash. We met at Highland Village off Northside Drive in Jackson. This time I was all business and no cheesing. I had to let it be known I ain't sweet-tempered and weak-willed. I might have been young, but this Lil baby was all about her Benjamins. This situation was way different from Mr. Lane. He wasn't performing surveillance on me, leading me and making sure I didn't get taken advantage of — my show, my rules, on my time.

I also knew I didn't intend on making the same bloopers I created before, squandering all my little bread until it was so low, I'd be backed against the wall again. Loving this new life, I lived only tempted me to take deals that guaranteed I kept this lifestyle.

My 'riding-around-town money' could pay most people's bills for a few months.

My taste had outgrown my bank account. Therefore, I needed to learn how to double or even triple my worth by investing. I knew I was dealing with a man who knew how to flip money. It was now my turn to talk.

"What should I do with this money?" I asked.

"Invest it," Mr. Mizkeli said. "Get a broker and buy some stocks. Spend it slow and do not deposit it in the bank. Go to the bank and get a safe deposit box." Mr. Lane put me on the safe deposit boxes. I just listened, pretending it was new news as he spoke.

"Get three at three different banks. You're going to be rich, think rich and act like it. A long way from the ghetto, huh?"

I interrupted him. "I'm not from the ghetto," I said. I was pissed off. No matter how much money I had or how many white neighbors I had, they still thought I was from the ghetto, but he was paying this black woman to kill his mom. That's ghetto.

I told Mr. Mizkeli to give me a week to get things in order. I wanted to take Mona on a trip before I moved into his mother's home.

I spent my last night at home thinking about what I had become. Then I realized I had my dream house. Instead of me cleaning a white person's house as a black woman, I was a young black woman getting my house cleaned by an older white woman.

Even though what I was doing was immorally wrong, it built one hell of a lifestyle. I believed I deserved this level of comfort.

Before I settled into bed, I decided to text Mr. Mizkeli. "See you in the morning!"

He replied with his mother's Eastover address.

ABOUT

THE AUTHOR

*L*aToya 'TOY' Lawson is a mystery author and caregiver whose creativity, compassion, and perseverance have all earned her the reputation as a service-centered leader. Born in Chicago and employed as a caregiver from the age of nineteen, LaToya 'TOY' Lawson has spent most of her life by the bedsides of the sick and infirm. By age twenty-three, she had founded Mississippi Professional Nursing Care, LLC, which would go on to inspire her debut novel, *MA'SITTER*. Through this career choice offered many rewarding moments, it was her lifelong passion to write that ultimately helped create this original work. As an African American woman living in Mississippi, TOY is familiar with the bigotry and social injustices of life in the deep south. An intensely personal work, the book was born from LaToya's firsthand experience with racism, faith, friendship and life as a single-mother in a world shaped by privilege. Her main character Victoria Lewis is a strong, single-minded woman, determined to build a better life for her child Mona. As a female writer Lawson's stories are at times filled with pain, but are ultimately uplifting, buoyed by the triumph and redemption of her characters.

When LaToya isn't writing, she can be found by her oven, checking her latest baked three-layer Red Velvet cake, or cooking a soul food feast and soaring down the highway on her motorcycle.